TIME AND THE CLOCK MICE, ETCETERA

TIME AND THE clockmice ETCETERA

Peter Dickinson

illustrated by

Emma Chichester-Clark

Delacorte Press

Published by Delacorte Press
Bantam Doubleday Dell Publishing Group, Inc.
1540 Broadway
New York, N.Y. 10036

This work was first published in Great Britain in 1993
by Transworld Publishers Ltd

Designed by Elizabeth Masters

Library of Congress Cataloguing in Publication Data applied for.

ISBN 0–385–32038–8

Manufactured in Portugal

May 1994

10 9 8 7 6 5 4 3 2 1

TIME AND THE CLOCK MICE, ETCETERA

START HERE

I prized the hatch loose. Inside was a deep hollow, with crank-rods running from the floor to pivots and joints near the top. On the floor, to the right of the rods, was a mouse's nest.

Now, you don't want mice in the works of clocks. They're dirty creatures, their droppings and leavings clog things up and they tend to gnaw around at random. I've often trapped mice, and put poison down, but when I've found actual nests with babies in them I've never been able to bring myself to destroy them.

The mother's run off, of course, so I scoop the nest up with the babies in it and tuck it away somewhere and hope she'll find it. Sometimes she does, sometimes she doesn't. I don't worry much, either way.

But this nest was different. For a start, the mother hadn't run off, though she must have heard me

forcing my way in. She was terrified, gazing up at me, quivering. She'd withdrawn her milk and her tiny blind babies were nuzzling uselessly at her teats.

The nest was the neatest I'd ever seen. The floor was so clean it might have been swept. Against the wall, near the rods, stood several of those plastic cylinders you buy camera film in. They held stores, bird-seed and raisins and bread-crusts.

And then I saw it wasn't just the way this mouse

did things that was different. *She* was different.

It was the eyes. If you look at an ordinary house mouse you'll see it has bright, slightly bulgy eyes. They look quick and cunning. But then you realize it's all on the surface. They're like shiny pebbles. You can't see into them at all.

But this mother mouse had stayed with her babies. She kept things tidy. She stored food in containers. And you could see into her eyes. They had depth, like people's eyes. We stared at each other for a long, long while.

'OK,' I whispered. 'Good luck with the family. Just don't let them muck around with the works.'

I inspected the cranks and pivots, gave them a touch of grease, closed the hatch and left the mother mouse to it.

So that's how I found out there were such things as Clock Mice. And that's how I knew from the first that they were different.

FIRST ESSAY ON MICE

The books say there are six kinds of British mouse.

They're wrong. There are seven.

The books will tell you about House Mice, which are very common. There must be millions of them. And about Wood Mice, which are the same as Field Mice, which are common too. So are Yellow-necked Mice. Harvest Mice used to be fairly common, but are getting rarer.

They'll tell you that Dormice aren't really mice, because they have furry tails and are halfway to being squirrels. They're getting rarer too.

The books will even tell you about Fat Dormice, which are pretty rare, but you'll know if you've got them because of the way they thump around in the attic. You can eat them, but the books don't tell you how to cook them.

That makes six kinds of British mouse.

The seventh kind is Clock Mice. They aren't in any of the books, because no-one has noticed them so far. They're very rare indeed – there were eighty-three last time I counted. They all live in the Branton Town Hall Clock.

They're different.

FIRST ESSAY ON CLOCKS

There are hundreds of kinds of clocks.

There are pendulum clocks and spring clocks and quartz clocks and water clocks and cuckoo clocks and Mickey Mouse clocks and turret clocks and lots and lots more.

The Branton Town Hall Clock is a turret clock. All that means is that it's a big clock in a tower, like a church clock. There are plenty of those. But there is only one Branton Town Hall Clock.

It's different.

SAT
MON
TUE
WED
THUR
FRI
NOV
JAN
FEB
APR
MAY
JUN
JUL
AUG
SEPT
OCT

Tourists come from the other side of the world to see it, and to photograph and film and video it as it strikes the quarters. It's pretty impressive even when it's not striking. It has dials which tell you the time of day (of course) and the date and the year and what the moon's doing and high tide at Branmouth Pier and where the planets are and when Halley's Comet is next due round and things like that, but what makes it really special is the way it strikes the quarters.

At fourteen minutes twenty seconds past the hour, six small bells tinkle a tune. A door opens on the right, below the moon dial, and two lambs

prance out on their hind legs, followed by a shepherd playing Pan-pipes, followed by Lady Spring in a yellow dress with a circlet of flowers in her hand, then another shepherd and two more lambs. They stop at the centre of the tower and twirl around while four bells strike the quarter, and then they begin to move away towards a door which has opened on the left.

But that's not the end of it. Before they reach the door, Old Father Time comes rushing out of the right-hand door with his scythe held ready to strike. He moves faster than they do, so you can see he's going to catch them just inside the door – in fact, his scythe is already swinging towards them as they all move out of sight. Tourists – people who've seen the Taj Mahal and the Pyramids and the Grand Canyon and the Great Wall of China – still gasp with amazement the first time they see the Branton Town Hall Clock strike the quarters.

(They bring a lot of money into Branton, those tourists.)

The half-hour and the three-quarters work the same way. Lady Summer wears a blue dress and has milkmaids and calves to dance with her. Lady Autumn wears gold and has harvesters and (I don't know why) rabbits. But Lady Winter . . .

She's magical, I think. She wears a cloak of green leaves and her face is as brown as a fallen leaf. Woodmen and foxes dance with her. Beyond

them waits a grim-looking man, also dressed in leaves, with a club in each hand poised above a drum. Inside the tower is a big bell called Old Joe, and as the hour booms out the man beats down on his drum at each stroke. Then Time comes out again and hunts them all into the dark.

That's the Branton Town Hall Clock. It's the place the Clock Mice call home.

SECOND ESSAY ON MICE

Most mice aren't clever. Rats are clever, as animals go, but mice are pretty thick. Sometimes House Mice will do something which seems clever, but that's because House Mice are crazy. They'll try anything, so sometimes they do something clever, by accident.

Clock Mice are different. They're really bright. Much brighter than rats, even. As bright as people.

They're bright because they have language.

It isn't a language like English or Spanish or Urdu. It isn't a language of eeks and squeaks, though Clock Mice can eek and squeak if they want to. Their real language is pictures. Pictures in their minds, which the other mice see in *their* minds, and then answer with their own pictures.

For instance, suppose Simon Dock . . .

Sorry, of course Clock Mice don't have that sort of name. They use pictures – nick-pictures, mostly. Miriam Dickory has slightly frizzy whiskers, so her family call her

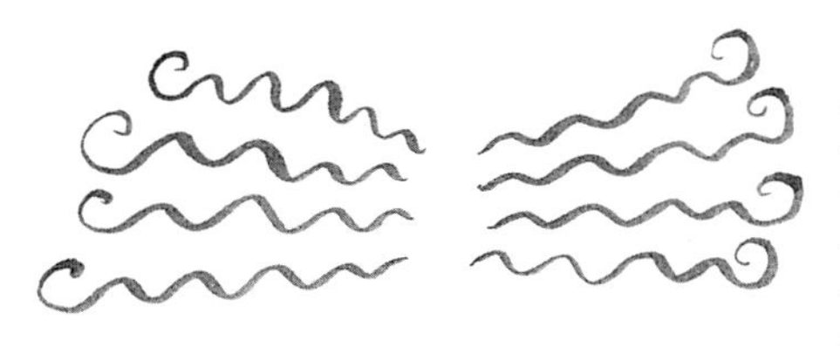

It's like calling a boy Curly because he has curly hair. But because I use word-language I've got to have word-names to talk about the different mice. There are three main families, so I called them the Hickorys and the Dickorys and the Docks. It's a bit obvious, I'm afraid, but I'm an old man and I can't change now.

Where was I?

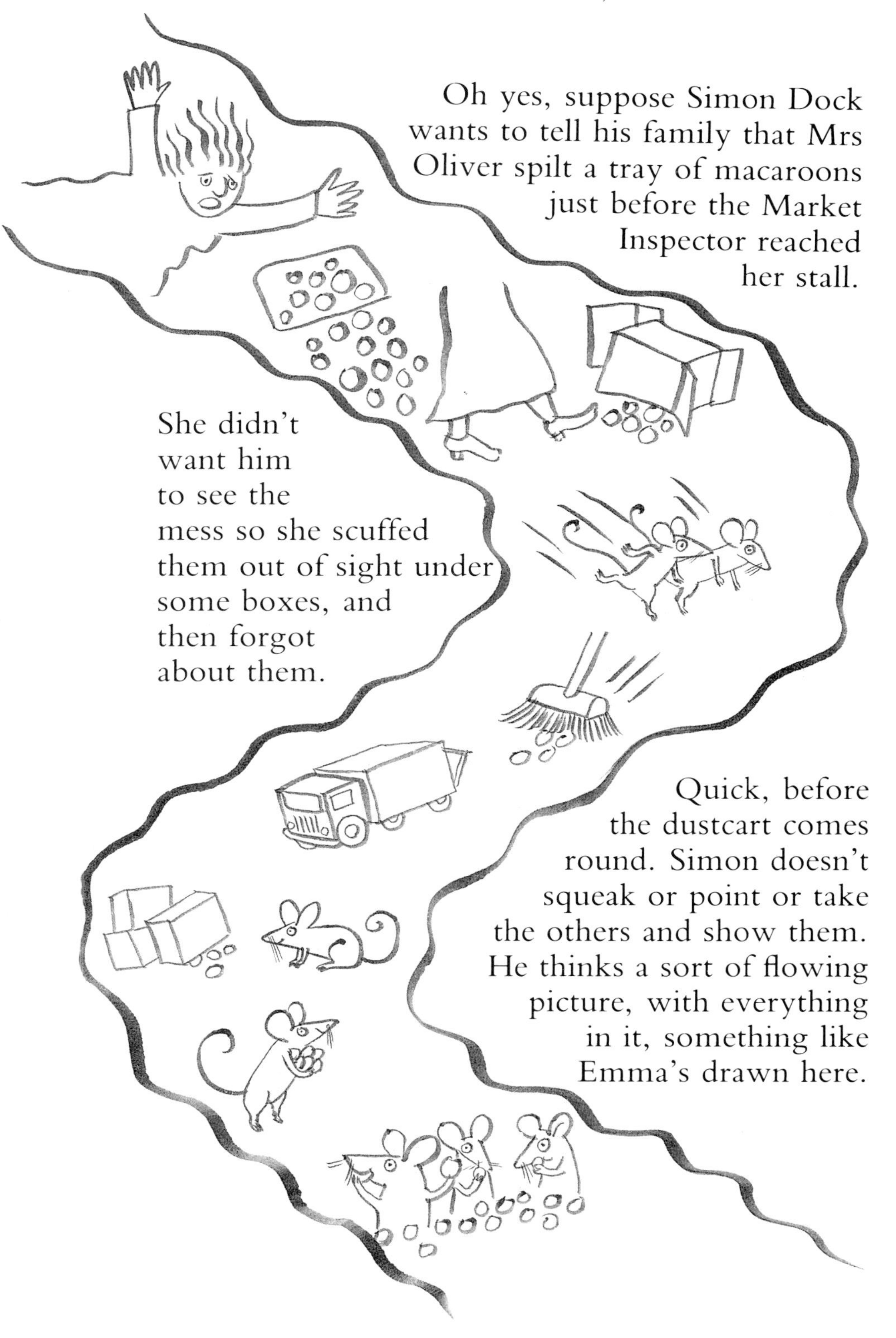

Oh yes, suppose Simon Dock wants to tell his family that Mrs Oliver spilt a tray of macaroons just before the Market Inspector reached her stall.

She didn't want him to see the mess so she scuffed them out of sight under some boxes, and then forgot about them.

Quick, before the dustcart comes round. Simon doesn't squeak or point or take the others and show them. He thinks a sort of flowing picture, with everything in it, something like Emma's drawn here.

Simon thinks quick and small, like whispering, because he doesn't want the Hickorys and Dickorys getting there first. Then suppose old Mavis Dock wants to say, 'Be careful! Where's Juno?' (Juno is the Town Hall cat. She's bright, for a cat, so she's dangerous. Later I'll tell you how she got Jeremy Hickory, though it was his fault, really.) Mavis can do that all in one go.

Clock Mice can put tones in their pictures, the way we do with our voices, if we're angry, for instance, or asking a question. The jagged edge round Mavis's picture shows it's a warning, and the wavy look on Juno shows it's a question – it's not really like that, of course, but it's the best we can do in a drawing.

(How do I know all this? How do I even know Clock Mice are as bright as people? I'll come to that later.)

Don't ask me how Clock Mice came to have this gift. Perhaps it isn't quite as extraordinary as it seems, because wild animals, especially the ones that live in groups, do seem to be able to let their companions know if they're angry or frightened or excited without making a noise or using other kinds of signals. They just feel it somehow. So maybe a cosmic ray hit the chromosomes of an ordinary mouse which happened to be living in the clock, so that that mouse's children were better at mind pictures and passed the gift on to their children, and so on . . .

That's the sort of scientific explanation I'd have given you a few months back, because that's the way I think.

But now, in spite of myself, I don't think it's like that at all.

I think it's got something to do with the clock.

SECOND ESSAY ON CLOCKS

Clocks are simple. And complicated.

They are complicated ways of using a simple idea.

This is the idea. All you need is something that happens at an exact speed, and a way of measuring it as it happens. The trouble is, not much happens at an exact speed, and most things happen too fast to be useful.

Drop a weight from an air balloon and it will fall faster and faster and faster, and hit the ground in less than a minute.

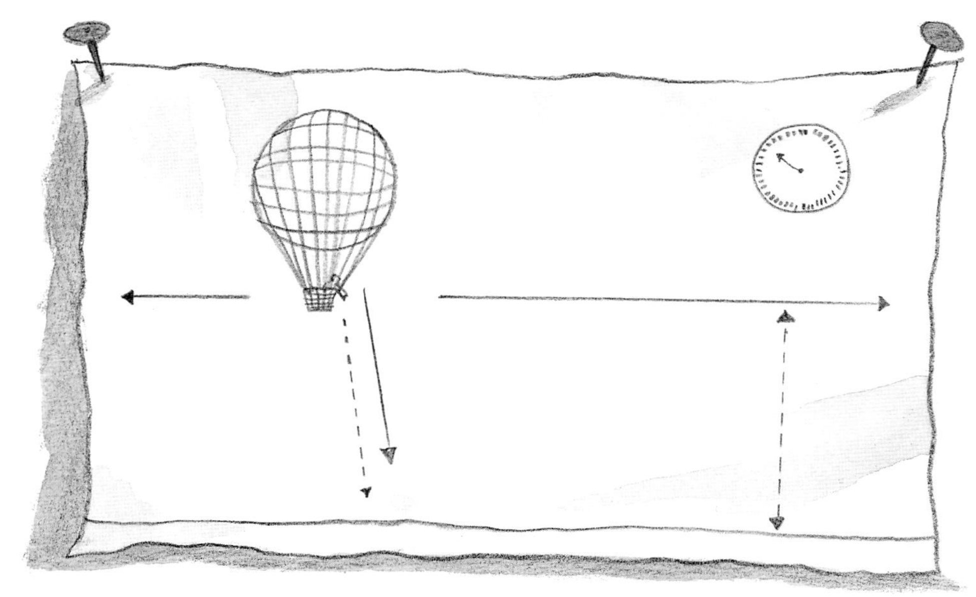

Not much use. You've got to make the weight fall slowly, and evenly.

So you hang your weight from a rope and you wind the other end of it round and round a drum. Now you've got to let the drum turn, but only slowly. You put a cogwheel at the end of the drum, and beside it you have a pendulum which swings to and fro. Pendulums swing at an exact speed.

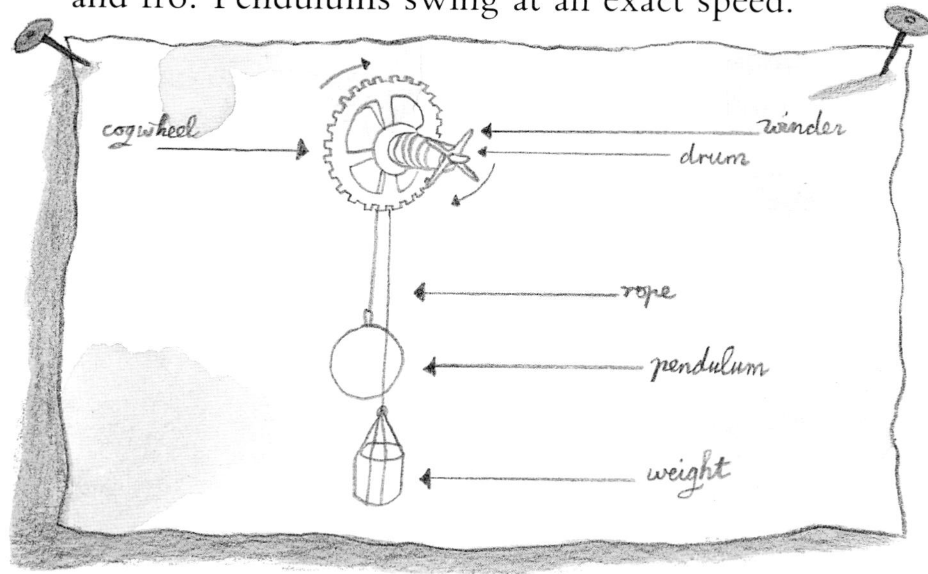

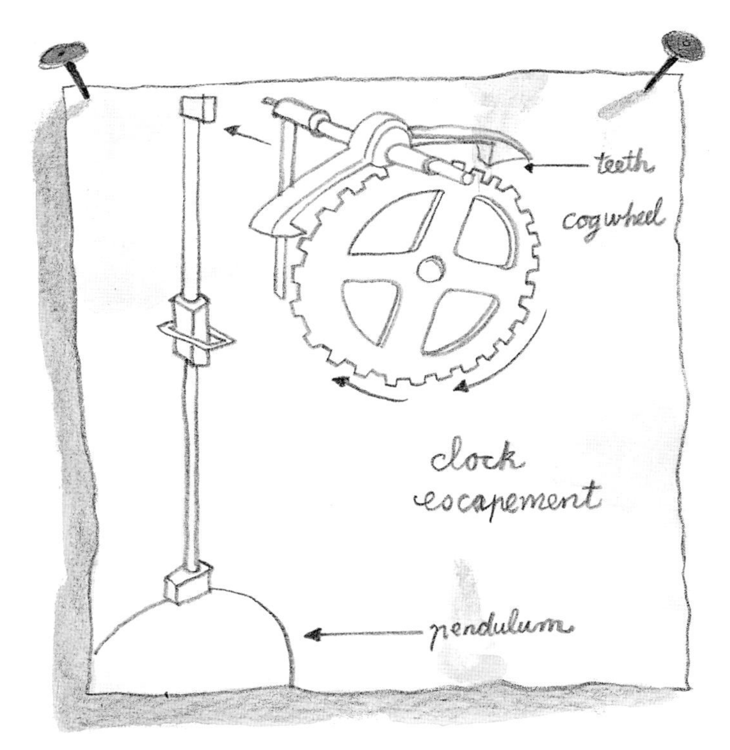

At the top of the pendulum you have a special-shaped arm with two teeth which fit into the notches of the cogwheel. At each swing this arm lets the wheel turn one notch, and at the same time the wheel gives the pendulum a shove so that it goes on swinging. That arm and wheel are the real heart of a clock. They're called the 'escapement'.

That's why clocks tick, and why the tick is different from the tock.

Of course, you need some more cogs to turn the hands and so on, but that's the basic idea of a pendulum clock.

The Branton Town Hall Clock is a pendulum clock. Bit by bit it's all very simple. Put the bits together and it becomes very complicated indeed.

It has ten weights. The ones that drive the dancers weigh over a tonne between them. I wind them all up. The pendulum swings. The hands go round until they almost reach one of the quarters.

Let's say it's the quarter-past. Inside the clock there's a wheel moving at the same speed as the minute hand. At twelve past, a peg on the side of this wheel reaches a lever and starts to push it. At fourteen past, plus twenty seconds, the lever flips over and turns a rod which releases a catch which has stopped one of the weights pulling down. Now, that weight drives a wheel which moves some hammers to strike the six small bells to ring their tune, and when it's finished it closes its own catch and releases two others, a small one to open the door and a large one to turn the carousel and bring Lady Spring and her team out into the open. (The carousel is a thing like a roundabout at a funfair, a big flat turntable with all the dancers on it.) As it stops it releases the catch that holds the other main weight, which turns the dancers. And so on.

Each bit of it is so simple that anyone could understand it. Putting all the bits together so that

they work with one another, and keep on working . . . Ah, that's another matter.

In fact, the Branton Town Hall Clock is so complicated that really, by rights, it oughtn't to go at all.

But it did. It ticked its slow tick and the quarters tinkled and Old Joe boomed the hours and the dancers danced and Time chased them away for the world to see until one day last year when, for the first time in all its ninety-nine years, the clock stopped.

The clock-keeper was a nice enough old boy called George Baff. He told the Town Clerk he'd done his best and anyway he wasn't feeling too good so he was going to bed. Luckily that happened when the tourist season was almost over, but everyone in Branton knew that they'd better get it going again. Next year was the centenary year, right? There could be a lot of money in that.

FIRST ESSAY ON PEOPLE

People want a lot. And even then they don't really know what they want.

Way back in 1893 the people of Branton thought they wanted a clock, so they asked my grandad to build them one.

He built them the Branton Town Hall Clock.

They said it wasn't what they wanted.

'It's too big,' they said. 'It's covered with fancy dials. Figures pop in and out and dance in a suggestive fashion. And that Father Time – depressing, he is. People will laugh at us, having a great big fancy clock in the Market Square.'

'It's a work of art,' my grandad told them. 'It's a Wonder of the World. There isn't another clock like it.'

'That's just the trouble,' they said. 'All we wanted was a clock like Yatterby has, and Sniffield, and Gloag, but you've gone and landed us with something like nobody else has got at all. It's not what we asked for, so we're not going to pay you.'

So Grandad went off in a huff. He took the plans with him.

My dad was never that interested in clocks. Airships were his thing. But I took after Grandad. Almost as soon as I could tell tick from tock I was hanging around his workshop. Before I was eight I'd built my first clock from two fruit-boxes and a few cogs and a weight from under his bench and the bell off my bicycle. Its hands went backwards and it ran for three and a half minutes, max, on a good day and it struck all the time it was running,

but it worked. It was a clock. And it made my dad realize he was never going to get me interested in airships, so he let me be apprenticed to Grandad when the time came.

Grandad never went back to Branton. He wouldn't let me go, either.

'I've shaken the dust of Branton off my shoes,' he'd say. 'I'm not going back till they send for me. That clock's not going to keep running for ever, and when it packs in there'll be no-one else can put it right.'

So he waited and waited and waited, and then he died.

He sent for me when he lay dying, and told everyone else to clear off. Then he got me to pull a chest out from under the bed.

'There's a green folder in there,' he croaked. 'That's the plans of the Branton Town Hall Clock. One day it's going to pack in, and there'll be no-one but you can put it right, because you've got the plans. All you've got to do is wait.'

Then he ate two pork pies and drank a glass of stout and died.

So I waited, and carried on my trade, making and mending clocks. It wasn't hard to get news of the Branton Town Hall Clock. It was always popping up on TV, when they'd nothing much else to finish a programme with. Then, one day last year, it was on the main news. First item was one of these princesses getting into another kerfuffle. Second was a war starting somewhere. Third was the Branton Town Hall Clock. It had stopped.

I sent a card to the Town Clerk, telling him I was the only one could get it going, because I'd got the plans. They sent one of these fax things back to Mrs Willink, who brought it round – that's how much of a hurry they were in.

I remember that first afternoon when the Town Clerk showed me round. The clock's got its own tower, a bit to the side of the Town Hall, looking over Market Square. The tower's not all that tall, just three storeys, though it looks like four from outside. The bottom floor's a big room where the WI sell cakes on Tuesdays and the Oxfam helpers sort clothes on Thursdays, and things like that happen.

You go up a winding stair in one corner into the weight room, which is double height, seven metres to the ceiling, to give the weights room to fall. Above that is what we call the going chamber, where the works are.

George Baff didn't come with us that day. He said he was still too ill, but as soon as I set foot in the weight room I saw why.

He was ashamed.

Now, George is a nice enough old boy, as I say. Maybe he's a few years younger than I am, but he still should have been old enough to know better.

I'd never seen anything like it.

What you find in an ordinary weight room is a big bare space with the pendulum going back and forth on the far wall and ropes looping down from the ceiling to the pulleys that carry the weights. Old days, the weights would be great lumps of stone, but by Grandad's day they'd gone over to what we call 'cheeses'. That's round slabs of iron with a slot in them so that you can pile them up round the rod that hangs from the pulley till you've got the weight you want.

George had piled all right. And when he'd got all the cheeses the rods would take he'd hung things on extra. They were like a scrap-iron dealer's dream of a Christmas tree, those weights, with anvils dangling off them, and great big iron cogs from abandoned mills, and cannon balls, and the odd bollard. An anchor even, he must have brought up from Branmouth. It's a wonder the beams above hadn't caved through, bringing the whole lot down,

works and carousel and bells and weights and all, on to the WI cakes below.

And the damage he must have done the old clock, bearings worn, rods buckled, levers out of true, pinions fractured, all to keep it groaning on another year because he didn't know how to set it right!

I didn't say anything. The room was haunted by silence, the ghost of a slow tick not there, because the long pendulum was still and the clock was dead.

Something scuttered across the floor above.

'We've got a few mice up there,' said the Town Clerk. 'They might be causing the trouble. George puts poison down, but they don't seem to take it.'

'Your trouble's never mice,' I said. 'Your trouble's people.'

THIRD ESSAY ON MICE

The Hickorys live at Spring, the Dickorys live at Summer and the Docks live at Autumn. None of them live at Winter. I used to think this was because they were scared of the foxes – foxes eat mice – but it isn't that. It's because it wouldn't be respectful to Lady Winter. I'll come to her later.

When Grandad carved the human figures he made them hollow, partly to save weight and partly because some of them have bits of machinery inside, so that Lady Autumn can wave her corn-dolly around and so on. They've all got to go out into the open once an hour, rain or shine, so he put drainage holes running down out of the hollow space through their legs and out at their heels, where you can't see them from below. The mice use these as their front doors.

I remember seeing Tracy Dickory when she was just out of the nest, sitting on the sill of one of the window-slits that let the bell-chimes

out. She was looking at the market closing down below, her nose twitching with interest. (She's a really bright, adventurous mouse, Tracy. In fact, she's the heroine of this story.) Then she noticed Sebastian Dock on the sill one along. In a flash she was off and round and up next door, asking him where he was from:

(That's a mousehole in a heel. The wavy look makes it a question. I'm not going to have to go on explaining this every time one of the mice asks a question, am I?) Sebastian answered:

(That's easy. He lives in the second harvester.) So Tracy knew he must be a Dock. The Docks don't get on with the Dickorys (or the Hickorys, come to that). The Dickorys say the Docks are snobs:

And the Docks say the Dickorys have fleas:

But Tracy's not the sort of mouse to worry about things like that. In three seconds she was chatting away about home life and her brother Kevin and how only yesterday morning when they were supposed to be asleep they'd sneaked up to their look-out place in their milkmaid's ear-hole and seen Uncle Gerald Dickory – a married mouse with great-great-grandchildren of his own – going sneaking off to meet Madeline Hickory behind the quarter-bells.

Sebastian was fascinated. That's not the sort of thing Docks talk about at home. Of course, like an idiot when he got back to the nest he let on what he'd been up to, and all the family insisted on searching him for fleas. He'll learn. And it didn't stop his Aunt Stephanie scampering round to tell her cronies what Madeline had been up to.

(All right. I made some of that up. I don't know exactly what Tracy and Sebastian talked about, but it would have been something like that. The rest of it's true.)

I've got a soft spot for Tracy, I admit. I must have seen her almost as soon as she was born. It was like this. I was having my first thorough look-round to see what needed doing so I could give the Town Clerk an estimate of what the job would cost. The original problem was the leading-off rods – they're the shafts that run out through the dials to turn the hands round. Because one end is out in the weather they tend to clog and rust and become stiffer to turn, so George had been hanging his extra weights on to keep them moving. I'd need scaffolding up the tower to get at them from outside, but that apart they

were no real problem. But there was no point, after George's efforts, in just dealing with them without putting the rest to rights.

Besides . . .

That clock was a wonder, all right. It was a young man's clock, romantic, impossible. Nobody but a young man in love with the sheer idea of time would have taken on building a clock on that scale, and knowing what I know now I don't think anyone but Grandad would have brought it off, and set it running for getting on a hundred years with no more than a spot of grease in the obvious places and the weight-ropes renewing every now and then.

I'd come to Branton telling myself I was going to teach them a lesson for what they'd done to Grandad, and by the time they'd finished they'd pay me what they owed him, twice over, but I hadn't been there more than a morning before I forgot about money. All I knew was that I was going to get Grandad's clock going again, no matter what, and set it running for another hundred years.

It took me a good two days to make my list of what needed doing, so it was towards the second evening before I took a look inside Lady Summer. I chose her because she was nearest. She'd got to raise an arm over her head while she was twirling, so on the plans there was a set of rods and pivots to see that happened. I found the inspection hatch in the carved folds of her dress between her shoulders. It can't have been opened for years, as the cracks had been painted over several times, but I managed to prize it loose . . .

(And now, if you can't remember what happened

on page 6 you're going to have to go back and read it again. I'm sorry. All that belongs in here, but they made me take it out and put it at the beginning. 'You can't start off with a *First Essay on Mice*, they said. 'Who's going to read a First Essay on anything? You've got to start with an exciting bit.' Ah well, I daresay they know what they're talking about.)

. . . I inspected the cranks and pivots. They were fine, so I gave them a touch of grease and closed the hatch and left the mother mouse to it.

It was getting late, but I opened up some of the other figures. Even the ones which didn't move their heads or arms had good big cavities in them, and all of them except the winter group had at least one family of mice living there.

One had a nest with babies. That mother stayed too. The other mice hid in the passage down to the entrance hole but I could see they lived there. All of the chambers had food-containers. Some had pieces of cloth on the floor, like carpets, and neat piles of bedding round the edges.

I closed the doors, sat down on my camp stool and finished making my notes. All around me I heard, or imagined I heard, faint movements as the mice crept back into their homes. They were frightened. I could feel their shared fright – I'm sure about that, just as I'm sure that when I switched off my light and went down the stairs I could feel their relief.

THIRD ESSAY ON CLOCKS

This essay is really about time, because I want to explain about mouse time being different, but I'll start with clocks.

Look at it this way. The time a pendulum takes to swing depends on its length. Give the bathroom light-pull a gentle shove and it'll swing, oh, a

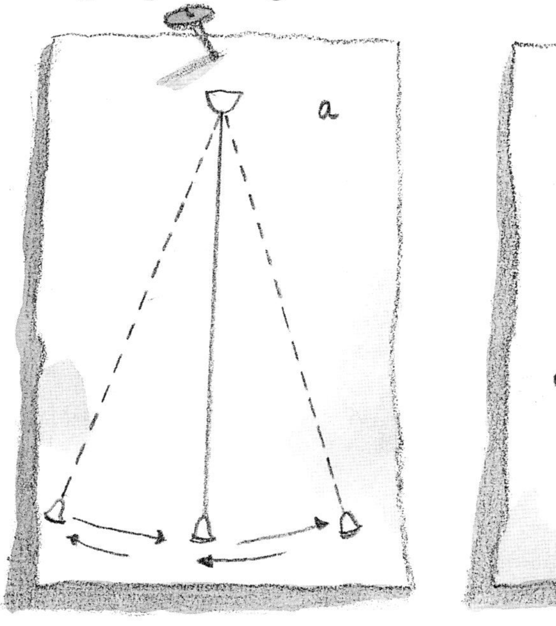

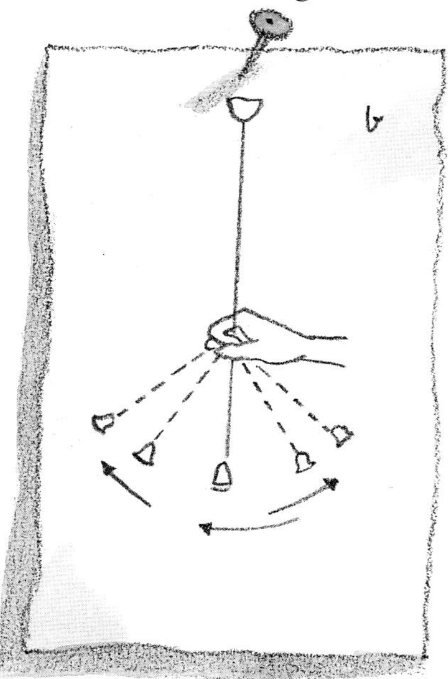

bit under once a second, depending how long it is. While it's still swinging take hold of it a little way from the bottom, and the swing of the loose bit will speed up. It's too light to make a proper pendulum, but if it had a decent weight on the end it would triple its speed, or more. A metre-long pendulum swings from tick to tock in half a second. The Branton Town Hall Clock has a four-metre pendulum, two seconds between tick and tock, the great, slow heartbeat that keeps it alive.

Animal hearts are like that, too. The larger the animal the slower the beat. A vole's heart beats twenty times as fast as an elephant's. (I'm not sure about the exact figures.) I've read somewhere that all mammals except humans live for roughly the same number of heartbeats, so an elephant lives twenty times as long as a vole. If humans were the same, twenty-seven would be a good old age for us. Perhaps it was, once, when we were still almost animals.

Where was I?

Oh, yes. Mouse lives seem short to us, but they aren't to them because they pack a lot in. They live at the speed of their heartbeats. If we could see life through a mouse's brain it would seem to whiz along like fast-forwarding a video. When I opened the back of Lady Summer I stared at Tracy's mum for about a minute, my time. She stared at me a good fifteen in hers. Ages.

They have babies quickly too. Healthy mice with plenty of food around can have ten litters a year. So why isn't the world waist-deep in squeaking furry

bodies? Because there isn't enough food, and lots of them get caught and eaten by other animals, and so on.

There's plenty of food in Branton Market and there's no-one to eat the Clock Mice except Juno, and they're usually too quick for her, so why isn't the clock tower crawling with brilliant telepathic mice?

First, they've slowed their birth-rate. They have two, or sometimes three litters a year, and they start breeding a bit later than ordinary mice. I suppose the parents have more to teach and the children have more to learn and understand, but I don't know whether this is something they've decided for themselves or something Nature's arranged for them.

Then there's another reason. If you look at a nest of the babies just after their eyes have opened, you can see that most of them aren't Clock Mice. There's always one or two (I've never seen more than three) which have eyes with the proper depth, that something-behind-the-surface, but the rest have pebble-eyes. The parents look after them all and feed them equally and seem just as fond of them.

Then, soon after they begin to run around,

the ordinary hard-eyed ones wander off and don't come back. It happens over two or three days. They go down to the market, and with all the food and scurry and excitement they just seem to forget about home. The parents don't drive them away, in fact they seem sad for a bit, and then they settle down to teaching the one or two who are left about life, and the world, and Lady Winter, and how not to get caught by Juno.

Apart from their own babies, until they leave, they won't let ordinary mice into the tower. They'll even gang up and drive off rats, though rats are much bigger and fiercer than they are.

Juno is another matter.

FIRST ESSAY ON CATS

You can't blame cats for killing birds and mice and baby rabbits. It's in their nature. They don't know the meaning of pity. I wish they wouldn't play with them first, but that's in their nature too.

SECOND ESSAY ON PEOPLE

People are different. There are plenty of things in *our* nature which you can still blame us for when we do them. Horrible things, sometimes, which we do to each other or to animals because the natural impulse is there, left over from before we were human. The difference is that we do know the meaning of pity. We can imagine what it's like to have such things done to one. We know that Nature's no excuse.

FIRST ESSAY ON CATS (continued)

I found out later that it was Dora McTurk who had let Juno up the stairs. It was Thursday, so the Oxfam workers were using the room at the bottom of the tower for sorting clothes. People coming to the market bring things that don't suit them after all, or they've got bored with, or their children have grown out of, or their aunts have given them, and the helpers sort them into what they can sell in Oxfam shops and what they can give to charity and what can only go for recycling and so on. I don't want to give the impression that Branton people are mean all through. They can be as generous as anyone about things they understand. Anyway, there the helpers were, all sorting away, when Jeremy Hickory tried to sneak through to the stairs.

It was all his fault. He should have been in bed long before the helpers came in, or at least found somewhere safe and waited till nightfall.

The fact is, he was drunk. It was a miracle he'd managed to find his way back to the tower, and now he'd got to cross this room full of helpers and piles of old jeans and wrong-size ski-pants and crazy headscarves and studded black biker jackets and so on. He was pie-eyed, reeling, smashed, and he wasn't used to it. He was a steady young mouse, really, but he'd married Fiona Dock a week ago and they'd had their first tiff last night, about whether they had to go round to dinner with the Docks every Wednesday for the rest of their lives:

(That's what Fiona said about dinner with her family.)

(And that's what Jeremy said.) And it had finished with Jeremy scuttling out, swearing.

As chance would have it, at the foot of the tower he'd found the broken bottom of a rum bottle with a drop of rum still in it – several stiff tots, if you're mouse-size – and Lady Winter knows what happened after that, but he'd been in a fight all right and his left eye was bunged solid and his fur reeked of female and that wouldn't be any of the Clock Mice. Oh, no. They were all accounted for.

Susan Hartley saw him first. She slung the moon-boot she was holding at him and missed. He made it under the pile of anoraks. Patty Biggs heaved them aside, and there he was in the open

again. Pete Wisley, who was helping his mother with the shoes, took a kick at him and sent him flying into the rack of evening dresses, but being drunk he landed without hurting himself. Janet Wisley came for him with a track-shoe but Wynnette Wynn, who can't bear to see an animal suffer, had tipped out a bin of baby socks and was rushing to trap him under the bin, screaming, 'Don't hurt it! Don't hurt it!' as she came. She crashed into Janet and brought the evening gowns down on both of them, and that gave Jeremy time to get his bearings and stagger off under the door at the foot of the stairs.

The helpers sorted themselves out. Dora McTurk waited till Wynnette had gone for her usual cup of herb tea. She fetched Juno who'd been having just as wild a night as Jeremy in her own cat fashion and was sleeping it off under the stove, unlocked the door to the tower and shoved her through.

'Go and earn your living, you lazy beast,' she said, and shut the door behind her.

FIRST ESSAY ON BELLS

There is something about bells. I think it's the way they go on humming to themselves after they've been hit and the main note has died away, but all sorts of other notes keep faintly coming and going. With a big bell, even after it's silent you can put your hand on the metal and feel the last tingle of vibrations, as though it were still singing to itself, private music of its own which we can't hear.

Maybe there's no more to it than that. Lots of things feel like mysteries, but aren't really. Maybe even time itself would turn out not to be mysterious at all if our minds were a different shape.

My cousin Minnie is into bell magic. She says that the universe is built on resonance, and a bell is a focus of the universal resonance which binds the electrons round the nucleus of an atom and the stars into their courses. Sounds good, doesn't it? A lot of nonsense sounds good, I'm afraid, but I'm fond of Minnie and she cooks great baps, so it was a good excuse to drive over to Witchwater Fell and see her when I decided that the C-sharp bell of the carillon didn't sound right. (The carillon's the tinkly tune before the quarters.)

Typical of Minnie to live at a place called Witchwater Fell. It's just a sprawl of old mining cottages up a hillside, most of them empty now. The Witchwater itself runs down a great pipe and drives turbines for electricity.

Minnie flicked at the bell with the middle finger of her left hand and listened to its note.

'That's a nasty, mean little bell you've got there,' she said. 'Lucky it isn't a big one. It could do a lot of harm if it were a big one.'

'I can't see it's cracked or anything,' I said.

'Ah, no,' she said. 'Cracked, and you can send them back to the foundry for re-casting. There's nothing you can do with a bell like you've got there. Melt it down and you'll infect a whole chime of bells that's cast from the one pot, and then you won't half have trouble in some unlucky parish.'

I didn't snort my disbelief, but I could afford to smile, Minnie being stone blind.

'I'll tell you what,' she said. 'I've got a sweet

little C-sharp bell I'll give you for your clock. You can have it for nothing, or nothing but this. Before the week's out you'll take the old bell down to Branmouth and you'll hire a boat and get them to run you a mile out to sea – two miles would be better – and you'll throw the bell over the side. That's all you can do with a bell like that. Only the sea's strong enough to take care of it. Now you can put it out of my house, right outside the garden gate, while I go and fetch you the other.'

Still smiling at her nonsense and looking forward to my baps I took the bell out and put it on the passenger seat of the van. When I came back up the garden path she was standing in the doorway with her own bell to her ear.

'I won't ask you in,' she said. 'You'd best be getting back. Someone's going to need you.'

'What do you mean?' I said.

'I don't know, but I can hear,' she said, and handed me the bell.

So I drove back to Branton with the old bell beside me and the new one in the back of the van. Maybe it should have been the other way round, because just as I was turning on to the motorway – a lorry had pulled out to let me in – a maniac in a Porsche swung into the slow lane and whizzed past at a hundred and twenty miles an hour, at least, not even sounding his horn till too late. How he missed me I don't know. My heart was still thumping when I reached the Branton turn-off.

No, of course it wouldn't have made a blind bit of difference which way round I'd had the bells. That's nonsense.

SECOND ESSAY ON CATS

Cats are a bit like bells, the way some people make a mystery of them when they haven't got one.

Cats just have that look, as if they knew what the old Sphinx knew, and they aren't going to tell us. I've another cousin, Cousin Angel, a good yard madder than Minnie and no kind of cook either, who actually worships cats. She keeps seven, called

Sunday, Monday, Tuesday and so on, and says her prayers to the one whose day it is. When one of them dies she looks for a kitten which was born as near as poss at the self-same instant, to take its place.

Cousin Angel knows the secret of the Sphinx. It goes like this.

Once cats ruled the world, and people were their slaves. The Sphinx was the great cat god. The books say that you find mummified cats in the tombs of the pharaohs. Wrong, says Cousin Angel. You find mummified pharaohs in the tombs of the cats. But then the cats did something absolutely frightful – Cousin Angel won't tell me what – but it was so frightful that the Sphinx laid a curse on them. They had to become the slaves of people for six thousand years. When the six thousand years are over they will start ruling the world again. Any day now, Cousin Angel says.

That's all nonsense, of course. Cats are animals, and the only secret they know is how to be cats.

I've got two cats of my own, called Lucy and Tompion. Lucy's black with bits of white, but the black's got a rusty look, as if it had been hennaed. Someone found her as a stray and gave her to me when my old cat died. She was pregnant, of course, and Tompion's the kitten I didn't manage to give away. There was a famous clockmaker called Thomas Tompion, so I thought it would be fun for me to have a tom called Tompion, but when I sent him to be neutered she came back spayed, so the joke doesn't work. She's black and white, and she's never got over being a kitten. Lucy jumps on my shoulders the moment I come down for breakfast, and would stay there all day long if I let her. Mrs Willink looks after them when I'm away. Where was I?

Oh, yes. There's no mystery about Lucy and Tompion. They're just animals. So is Juno.

I must have got back about five minutes after Dora McTurk put Juno up the stairs. Wynnette Wynn was back from her tea-break, so Dora couldn't warn me without upsetting her. The first I knew of it was the racket I heard the moment I got into the weight room. It came from the floor above. I never heard such scurryings and squeakings. If the Oxfam people hadn't been doing their own sort of scurrying and squeaking they'd have heard too. It was almost noon, the middle of the night from a mouse point of view. They should all have been asleep.

I went quick as I could up the stairs and peeped round the door. Juno had her back to me. She was playing with Jeremy before she killed him, the way cats do – or at least she was trying to, because she was having trouble keeping her mind on the game. All the adult mice, Hickorys and Dickorys and Docks, and never mind the family feuds, were doing their darnedest to interfere.

They were rushing about the floor, darting in front of Juno, squeaking like maniacs, hither and thither, criss-cross, just out of reach, daring her to have a go at them. I was still watching in amazement, trying to work out what was going on, when she pounced. The mice scattered for cover. Their idea was to give Jeremy a chance to get away while Juno was chasing them, but there was something wrong with his front legs and he could barely move.

Juno must have had a few goes at them already and missed, but as I say she's bright for a cat, and this time she'd made allowances and picked her target. She got Emily Dickory's tail just as Emily was slipping out of sight under one of the carousel-beams.

I nipped into the room and popped Minnie's bell over Jeremy so that Juno couldn't get at him, in case I failed to catch her first go, but I was wearing sneakers and she didn't hear me coming above all the eeking and squeaking. I grabbed her by the scruff

of loose skin between her shoulder-blades. Lord, I was angry! No point, really – Juno was doing her job, and Dora McTurk had behaved quite sensibly, to my mind – much more so than Wynnette Wynn would have. Luckily I didn't know then how Juno had got in, so I couldn't start yelling at the Oxfam helpers. I just opened the bottom door, dropped Juno through, closed it and went back up the stairs.

The mice were waiting for me. I couldn't see them, but I could feel them, all round the going chamber, peering out from the darkness under the carousel, from the ear-holes of the dancers, from the ledges of the bell-frame, waiting to see what I'd do.

As soon as I lifted Minnie's bell Jeremy tried to crawl for safety, but Juno had broken both his front legs so all he could do was shove his front end along the floor with his back legs. It must have been agony.

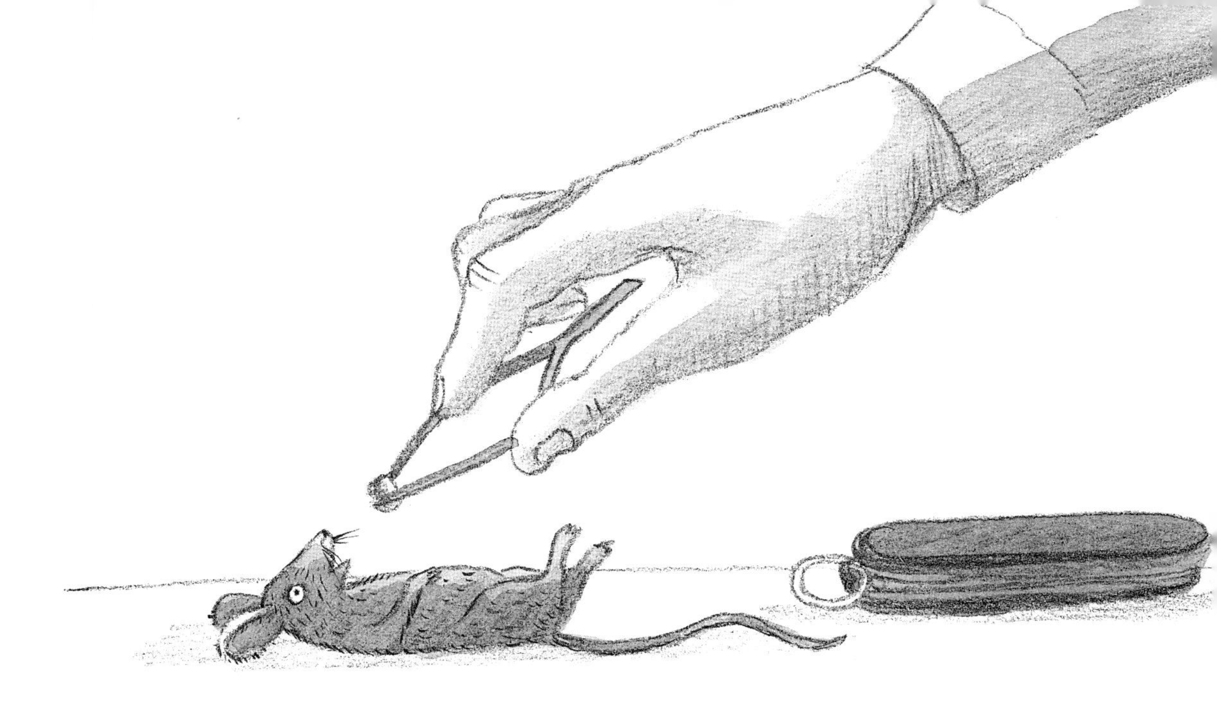

I picked him up and laid him on his side on my Work-mate and made signs to him to lie still. I get the odd headache so I usually carry aspirin. I fetched out a tablet, chipped a crumb of it off with my Swiss knife and used the tweezers to put it in Jeremy's mouth. I had to guess the quantities, but I've done the sums since and reckon I gave him about as much as eight tablets would have been for a human. He pretty well passed out and I was able to set his legs, using matchsticks for splints and tying them firm with strips I scissored from my handkerchief.

It was tricky work with clumsy great human fingers. I had to use my reading-specs and really concentrate, but after a bit I noticed a movement out of the corner of my eye. Fiona, Jeremy's wife, was sitting there, quiet as a . . . well, as a mouse, I suppose, watching me work.

I moved my hands aside and she crept over and sniffed at his hurt legs and combed his whiskers, thinking sorry thoughts at him:

Then she moved back and let me finish the job. When it was done I opened the back of the first shepherd and lifted Jeremy into my hand and let Fiona climb up beside him and carried them back to their home and put them safe inside.

I dare say Fiona gave him a good thinking-to when he came round from the aspirin:

Next morning I drove to Branmouth and hired a boat and got myself taken five miles out, beyond the old sea-wall, and dropped the other bell over the side into deep water. I knew it was a lot of nonsense, really, but I felt I owed it to Minnie. I didn't ask the boatman what he thought. None of his business.

FOURTH ESSAY ON CLOCKS

Getting an old clock going is an art. It's all a matter of balance, really. The pendulum, for instance . . .

It's got to hang level. Take an ordinary grandfather clock in a case. It's no use levelling up the case with a spirit-level – a lot of cases have got a bit warped and worn over the years. It's not even the main frame that holds the works. It's just the way the pendulum swings in the escapement – that's the bit Emma drew for my *Second Essay on Clocks*, which lets the hands turn at a steady rate and at the same time gives the pendulum a shove to keep it going.

What you've got to do is wind the clock up, swing the pendulum to one side and let it go.

And listen.

The first few ticks you won't hear anything useful. Then, as the swing settles you begin to tell. What you're after is a steady, even beat, each tick the same distance from its tock as the tock is from its tick. You can fiddle around with the levels, or sometimes there's a bit of soft wire you can bend in the arm which carries the swing of the pendulum up to the escapement, until you've got the beat healthy.

Once you've got it right you can wind your clock up Sunday by Sunday – after church and before roast meat as my grandad used to say, though I'm not a churchgoer myself, but that's still the right time for clock-winding – and it will run for thirty-odd years with no more looking-to.

But some clocks, alter their level by as little as sliding a playing-card under one side of the works, and they'll die on you. Others, you can pretty well heave around the room every time you feel like shifting the furniture, and they'll keep going. That sort have got a lot of what we call tolerance.

Now, I'm putting this in because there's something important about the Branton Town Hall Clock. It had negative tolerance.

It shouldn't, by rights, have gone at all.

The more I worked at it, and the more I eased and cleaned and tightened and straightened and replaced, and the more I stared at Grandad's plans, the more puzzled I became.

An ordinary simple clock doesn't need a lot of tolerance, because there's not that much to put it out of balance, but a great, fantastic mechanism like the Branton Town Hall Clock needs a mass of tolerance in every separate part of it, because of the way all the parts are likely to work against all the others. A little bit wrong here, a little bit wrong there, and whoops, you've got a stopped clock.

But I tell you, for instance, that if you'd slid a sheet of tissue paper under one of the main beams that carried the going train (supposing you could) the pendulum swing would die on you. And the same all over.

And yet my grandad had built the clock in 1893 and it had run on, rain and shine, getting on a hundred years without much help from the likes of George Baff, until the day it stopped.

I couldn't make it out. In fact, by the time I made my trip up to Minnie to swap the C-sharp bells I was having my doubts whether I'd ever get it going, even after I'd set everything to rights. But from then on things changed.

I'm not saying it was anything to do with the actual bells, though Minnie'd tell you that, I dare say, but bit by bit as I worked I began to see how Grandad had balanced one lot of problems against another, and got them to cancel out. Something a bit out of kilter here would balance itself against something maybe a little wonky there, just coming in at the right moment, on the exact tick or tock where it was needed. It wasn't anything I could see from the plans, only as I worked with my hands, waiting for the moment when the job *felt* right, and then leaving well alone. Like listening for a healthy beat from the pendulum.

It's all a matter of balance, as I was saying. That's important, because, well, I still don't know how, but maybe the mice are part of it.

I was seeing a bit more of them after Jeremy's adventure. Not all the time, of course, them being night-creatures and me being a day-creature, but they had their comings and goings even by day, and now they weren't bothered about me being aware of them. Myself, I wasn't going to presume on me having popped up at the right moment to help Jeremy, so I didn't go prying into their houses except when I needed to deal with the works in some of them. Then I always took the trouble to knock.

I kept an eye on Jeremy while his legs mended, seeing the splints stayed firm till I could have them off. It took about ten days for that, him living in mouse time. I'd made a fair enough job of it, though he'll limp on his left leg for the rest of his days.

Funny thing. Fiona and Jeremy hit it off with each other a good bit better than they looked like doing before. Fiona likes the idea that her Jeremy was mouse enough to take on the market mice in a brawl, and you should have seen what she said to her mother about showing him proper respect from now on:

A different sort of funny thing. Midwinter night I was working late, because I'd promised myself I'd have the striking-train for the hours sorted out before I knocked off for Christmas. I was still at it, getting on nine o'clock, when the mice began stirring. I imagined they'd just be getting going for a good night's foraging, but instead of that they all began gathering on to the carousel round Lady Winter's group. They came family by family, all of them carrying something, nuts and raisins and other bits and bobs of food they must have been saving. They didn't scuttle and dart, the way mice do, but went steadily, all together, and there wasn't an eek or a squeak even from the littlest ones.

I thought my lights might be bothering them, so I switched them all off except the inspection lamp over my Work-mate and went on with what I was doing, just glancing their way every now and then.

It was hard to see in the shadows, but as far as I could make out they piled their little offerings round Lady Winter's feet and decorated them with shiny bits they'd brought up from the square – plenty of stuff like that around, with the stall selling Christmas decorations. Then they made a circle round her and did nothing. (I won't ask Emma to draw what they were thinking – I don't see how.)

Twenty minutes on – an hour and more in mouse time – they began to stir again. I heard scufflings and nibblings and an eek or two from the young ones. Then Fiona – I hadn't heard her coming – popped up on to the Work-mate with a peanut in her mouth. She put it down and nudged it towards me with her nose.

I could see what was expected of me, though I wasn't that keen on eating what a mouse has had in her mouth, so I took a chance and chewed it up. She looked up at me for a few seconds. I didn't know then, of course, but she must have been thinking thanks:

Then she scampered away.
I fetched a chocolate digestive from my dinner-box – I'm partial to them between meals – and broke it up and took it over and laid it down with the other food at Lady Winter's feet, where the mice were having their Midwinter Feast, or whatever it was. Old Hiram Dickory fetched the biggest bit back to his place at once. Greedy old snuffler, I was thinking, but he took no more than a nibble

and passed it on to his left, and it went on round the circle like a loving-cup till it was finished and they fetched themselves another piece to carry on with.

When I came back after Christmas I took a look at the carousel. There wasn't a crumb to be seen where the mice had held their feast. It could have been swept by a careful housewife, it was that clean.

SECOND ESSAY ON BELLS

The bigger the bell, the deeper the note.

The Branton Town Hall Clock has eleven bells, six small ones for the carillon, four middle-size ones for the quarters, and Old Joe for the hours. The carillon tinkles, the quarters sing and Old Joe booms. On a good day with the right sou'wester blowing, people hear him in Gloag, nine miles off across the moors. The cliffs at Chough Scaur funnel the sound along, apparently. I wouldn't know.

The carillon came from the old steam merry-go-round which Grandad bought and converted to make the carousel. The quarter bells were cast for the clock, special. Old Joe came from the church of St Joseph Beyond, which was drowned when the sea-wall gave in the great storm of 1748.

They'll tell you at Branton that the young priest at St Joseph's rang that bell all night through during the storm. There were rich farmers all across the drained lands, but their minds were on their own acres and the wall had stood storms before, so they never saw reason to spend money on it, let alone on the church beside it and the poor priest who served there. He'd been out on the wall that evening getting his lines in so that he could have a mackerel or two for tea when he felt the wall beginning to move beneath his feet with the onset of the storm, so he'd skipped tea and gone to the church to set Old Joe ringing.

The sound of the bell was carried on the wind as it rose and gusted across the drained lands. In the full roar of the storm the people of the farms woke and heard Old Joe clamouring his warning along the wind and knew they had to clear out. In the length and breadth of the drained lands not a human life was lost on that dreadful night, thanks to Old Joe and the priest.

The wall gave and the sea came hurling through, carrying all before it. The body of the church, which was timber, was washed away, but the stone tower stood and the priest worked his way up it as the water rose, floor by floor, keeping the bell-rope going. When the storm cleared and they rowed out looking for cattle and such which might have made it to the parts of the wall still standing, they found the priest at the bell-chamber window, good as dead from cold and hunger and exhaustion.

Soon as he was ashore and rested he had them send out to rescue Old Joe before the tower gave way. They owed their lives to the bell as much as to the man, he said. He must have been a good man, as well as a brave one, for though he was stone deaf for the rest of his days from Old Joe's ringing he came to be Archbishop of York despite that.

(I don't swear all of that's true, but it's what they'll tell you in Branton.)

Now I'd sent Cousin Minnie a Christmas tape, cards being not much use to her, telling her how I was doing. Our family's not much on seasonal chat, but she called me Boxing Day to thank me, and almost the first thing she said was, 'What did you do with that nasty little bell?'

'What you told me,' I said. 'I got the fellow to run me out beyond the old sea-wall, so I could drop it in open water.'

'That should do,' she said. 'I've been fretting about that bell. It was wickeder than I'd thought, somehow. I can't see why it didn't do more harm than it seems to have done. What are the other ones like?'

'They sound all right to me,' I said.

'I'd just like to come and have a look,' she said.

(Blind people say 'look', like that, without noticing. It always seems a bit queer, though I don't know what else they could say.)

'You're welcome,' I said. 'I'll get the diary and see when I can come over and fetch you.'

'No you won't,' she said. 'I'm coming on the buses.'

It's three buses, with a forty-minute wait at Yatterby, but Minnie likes to show she doesn't depend on anyone. She came over second week of January. Brought me some baps, too.

Soon as we were into the going chamber she stood still, just listening. Then she tapped her way forward. She seemed to know where the bells hung without being told and she worked her way round to them, tapping her stick against the edge of the carousel. There's ropes and rods and cranks

running at floor-level, but she found them all and stepped over.

The carillon bells hang in a line, with the quarter bells beyond, but Old Joe's right on round the other side, all by himself. It's because there's not room for three lots of striking-chain weights over beyond the big carousel weights, so Old Joe's hangs with the ones belonging to the main going-train.

Minnie worked along the bells, first holding her hands just clear of them as if she was warming her fingers, then flicking them with the middle finger of her left hand, and going on listening long after any sort of sound had gone that I could hear.

That's more like it,' she said, when she got to the C sharp. 'That's an honest little bell you've got now.'

She tapped on round to Old Joe and did her finger-warming trick.

'Ah,' she said, and struck him with her whole fist.

Now I've tried that, and I can't get a sound out of him. There's too much mass there to vibrate until he's hit by something hard and heavy as his own hammer. But when Minnie struck him with her soft-looking little white fist he crooned for her, a soft, deep, quivering note that changed and wandered.

She stood listening and nodding her head.

'That's why,' she said at last. 'There wasn't much that nasty little bell could do with a bell like this around. I won't explain to you. You think it's all nonsense, but I was bothered about you getting home safe that day.'

'I near as toucher didn't,' I said, and told her about the maniac in the Porsche.

She was tapping her way on round the carousel towards the door when she stopped and stood still as if someone had called her name.

'Who's there?' she said, sharply.

'It's only Lady Winter,' I said. 'You're right alongside of her.'

She knew what I was talking about because I'd explained in my tape about the dancers. She turned and held her hands close to the carved wood, the way she'd done with the bells.

'I see,' she said. 'Oh, yes, I do see.'

'What was all that about?' I said as I was helping her down the stairs.

She wouldn't tell me.

'You think it's all nonsense,' she said. 'Only don't forget we're first cousins. He was my grandad as well as yours.'

FIRST ESSAY ON SCIENCE

There's always more than one sort of explanation for things. Anything worth explaining, that is.

I remember Grandad giving me two Swiss rolls and telling me to slice them up, one longways, one crossways. Longways I got straight stripes on the slices, and crossways I got spirals.

'How do you get both on the same slice?' he said.

'You don't,' I said, after I'd thought about it.

'Right,' he said, and we took the cakes off to the park to feed the ducks with. (They were stale already, I should have said, left over from Cousin Ivy's wedding which she didn't turn up at.)

Science is just one way of slicing the cake.

I thought about this sometimes while I was working at the clock, after Cousin Minnie's visit. The work went well, hardly a hitch, provided I kept at it honestly and didn't try any short cuts.

That's the point. Maybe there *was* something special and strange about the clock, and Old Joe, and Lady Winter – the sort of thing Minnie believed in and I didn't, and that's why the clock had kept going all those years when by rights it should have stopped.

That didn't affect me. The clock had stopped for perfectly good everyday reasons, such as the leading-off rods being let rust up, so it was no good me sitting back and expecting Minnie to hocus-pocus it going again with her bells. The scaffolding came third week in January, and mother, was it cold up there with the north-east wind whipping the snow-flurries off the fells. So it was up to me to get the hands off and ease the leading-off rod back, and cut and fit new bushes and re-true the rod, and the same with all the other dials, while Hiram and Solomon Kapo – nice lads, both – painted the dials fresh.

And the same all through, pulleys and ropes and levers and pinions and the big tapering rollers that carried the carousel by way of bearings. I'd got to get them working by the ordinary laws of classroom science, or all the resonance in the universe wouldn't make a single tick lead on to its tock.

The same with the mice. Maybe there was something wonderful about them, and Lady Winter, and maybe Old Joe had something to do with it, but I began to think there was a perfectly simple everyday reason why they had to be there, and the clock wouldn't go without them. I was fiddling with the train for the Halley's Comet dial – fancy bit of cam-work, that has, to show the orbit – and I needed Solomon on the scaffolding outside to give it a bit of a biff in the right place, so I opened up the grille over one of the slit windows so I could lean out and sign to him what I wanted.

As I was closing up again I noticed the grille had been mended in one corner, with a bit of thin

wire woven in. Not by George Baff, or any human, though. It had never been twisted tight with pliers, but it had been, like I say, woven firm, the way a mouse might weave its nest firm.

That set me thinking. A place like the Branton Clock Tower, with the market so close below, what would you expect to find? Rats, mice, pigeons, starlings – starlings are devils for pecking their way into where they fancy nesting – not to mention beetles and bugs. There'd be droppings everywhere, rinds, scraps, bits of old nest, feathers, dead bodies, mostly just lying around harmless, apart from the stink, but every so often a bit of something wrapping itself round a rod, or tumbling into a shaft, or lying against a lever – just the sort of thing to stop a clock that's anyway on the edge of not going at all.

But the mice didn't allow anyone in to make that kind of mess, and they cleaned up their leavings almost well enough to please my Cousin Elsie, who feather-dusts her ornaments three times a day. It was just as if they were proud of their clock, took an interest in it. If there'd been a Branton Town Hall Clock Preservation Society they'd have been founder members.

Tracy took more than an interest. Most of the mice, as I say, I didn't see a lot of, but Tracy was different. I don't know what the rest of them felt about the clock being stopped. It didn't affect them much, though it had finally stuck during the three-quarter strike, but George Baff had had the sense (I'll give him that) to crank the carousel round and bring Lady Autumn and her lot (and the Docks too, if he'd known) in out of the weather. So they went about their business much as before. A bit more restfully, I dare say, without their homes facing a new way each time the carousel moved and Old Joe juddering them out of their nests whenever he boomed the hours.

But Tracy wanted to know what I was up to. She was really interested. She'd perch on the bench close as she could get (mice are short-sighted, by our standards) and follow every detail. If I had a chocolate biscuit to keep me going through to the next meal I'd give her a corner and she'd eat it, but

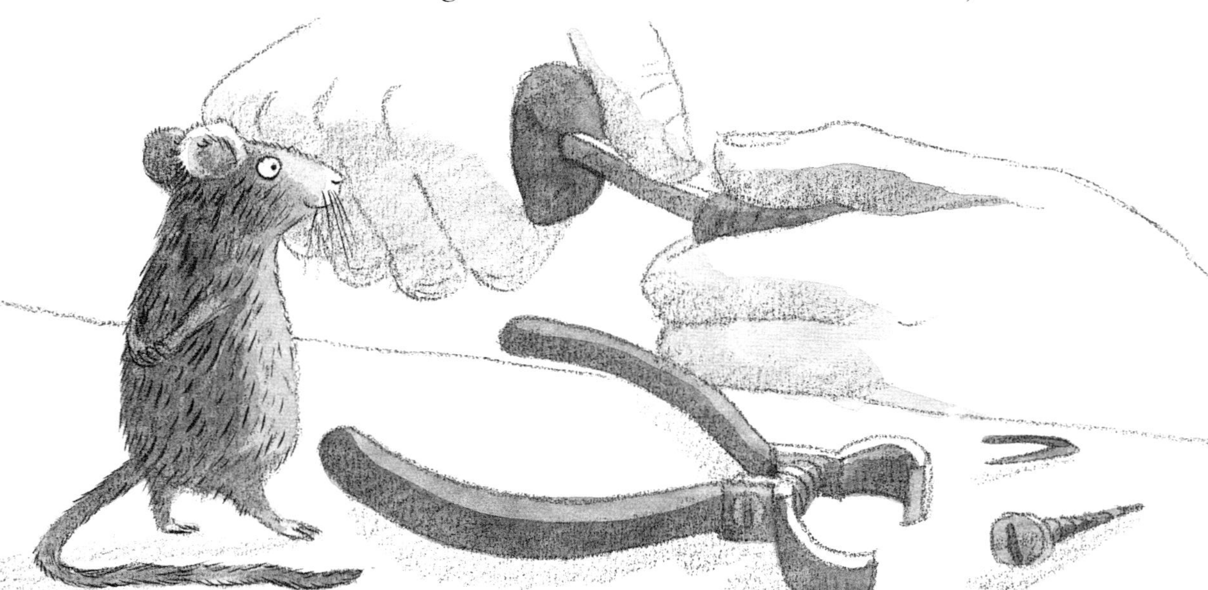

she didn't come nosing into my pockets looking for more the way a pet mouse would have, and as soon as I started work again there she was, studying and thinking, so close sometimes that if I was straightening a rod I could actually smell the scorch of her fur from the red-hot metal. She wasn't scared of the roar of the blowlamp. I had to get a spare set of goggles so she could sit behind one of the eye-pieces and watch me welding.

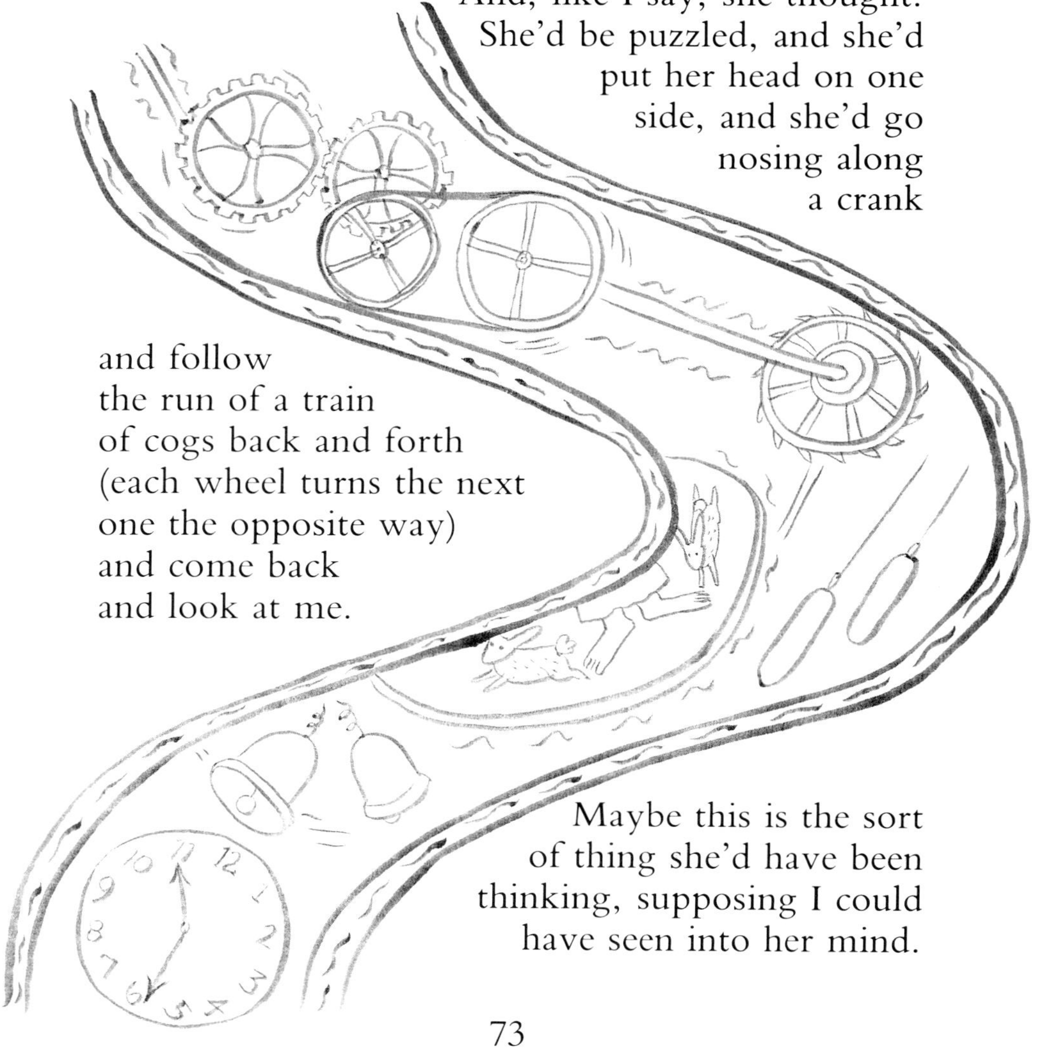

And, like I say, she thought. She'd be puzzled, and she'd put her head on one side, and she'd go nosing along a crank and follow the run of a train of cogs back and forth (each wheel turns the next one the opposite way) and come back and look at me.

Maybe this is the sort of thing she'd have been thinking, supposing I could have seen into her mind.

But even without that I could tell she'd got it.

She hadn't been born when the clock stopped. She was a naked pink slug at her mother's teat, remember, when I'd first opened the hatch in Lady Summer's back, October some time. Maybe some of the older ones had told her about how in the old days the carousel used to go round and round and the bells would tinkle and clang and boom – the way we talk about the old days when there wasn't any television and people made their own amusements – so maybe she'd some idea what all that machinery was for. But she'd never seen it going.

She worked it out though, bit by bit.

Though we couldn't say a word to each other, I came to have a real fellow-feeling for Tracy. When I'd come to Branton there was only me in the whole world who knew how the Branton Town Hall Clock was supposed to work.

Now there were two of us.

THIRD ESSAY ON PEOPLE

People are clever, but they don't like thinking. Not for themselves. Ready-made thoughts are what they like.

My Cousin Duncan makes a living out of this fact. He cuts mottos on pin-heads and sells them, everyday true sayings like *There's no place like home* and *Mother knows best* and *It is Father's fault.* I can't think why anyone should buy them. You need a powerful magnifying glass to read the message, and then it turns out to be something you knew already. Pin-heads appeal to pin-heads, I told him once, and he wasn't pleased, but next time I see him I'll tell him I'm sorry and ask him to carve one for me, special.

There's no fool like an old fool.

It was the champagne did it. That, and the bright, admiring eyes with their long curling lashes, and the pretty little red, red mouth.

And being too pleased with myself.

I'd reason to be pleased, mind you, because everything had gone so well, better than I could ever have dreamed. The business with the carousel bearings just topped it all off.

I'd been bothered about them all along. Very first time I'd looked at the clock I'd cranked the carousel round a notch and found it took all my strength to move it, while it groaned like far-off thunder. No wonder George Baff had been hanging anvils on its weights. The bearings were gone.

I'd borrowed a few jacks from the bus-depot and got them under and jacked the whole thing up and found what I'd been afraid of. The bearings were tapered rollers, twelve of them, half a metre long, ten centimetres wide at the fat end and six the other, running in a nest-shaped track, with the whole carousel balanced on them and steadied by wheels out at the edges.

They were box-wood.

Where do you get ten-centimetre section box, six metres of it, true, knotless, in this day and age? I asked around pretty well every specialist timber merchant in the country. Not a hope. So in the end I had a set turned for me out of some kind of foreign hardwood. They looked all right, but they didn't feel all right. It was the best I could do, but I wasn't happy. It wasn't what Grandad had used.

Then a week before I was going to start putting the whole thing back together I saw my Cousin Cyrus on TV. We'd not been on speaking terms most of our lives, due to a disagreement about home-made marmalade when we were both young

and hot-headed, but we'd made it up a couple of years back while we were letting off the fireworks at Cousin Dennis's funeral. (That was a party!) Not that he'd been right about the marmalade, but there comes a time when you can let bygones be bygones.

Cyrus was always crazy about trees, but they take him seriously these days, outside the family at least. He's become a world expert on rainforests, so he's not often in the country, but there he was on TV so I rang him up to say welcome home. In the course of telling him what I'd been up to I mentioned my dealings with the timber merchants, because I thought he'd be interested.

'You'd much better stick to box,' he said.

'I can't get box, I told you,' I said.

'I'll look in the back of my shed,' he said.

'I tell you I need six metres of true, knotless, seasoned, ten-centimetre finish box,' I said. 'You won't find that in the back of your shed.'

'What'll you bet?' he said.

'I'll eat a pot of your rotten sweet marmalade.'

'It's a deal.'

'And I've got to have them Tuesday, latest.'

'Just give me the exact measurements.'

And next Tuesday, sure enough, I was looking at twelve box-wood rollers, turned, waxed and polished, and a pot of marmalade I'd once sworn I wouldn't eat to save my life on a desert island. It was a three kilogram pot, too.

The carousel settled on to the rollers as if it had known them all its life, and turned with barely a whisper. The whole job had gone smoothly which was why it was finished three weeks ahead of schedule. I'd call to be pleased.

But I shouldn't have been pleased with myself.

You could put that on one of Cousin Duncan's pin-heads. *Be pleased, but not with yourself.*

It was just luck, things going so sweetly, and once you start taking credit for your luck you're in for trouble. Fact.

I told the Town Clerk, and maybe he didn't believe me, so he insisted on coming along early one Sunday morning before anyone was up, to see the clock going. At five to six I lifted the bob of the pendulum sideways along the wall of the weight room

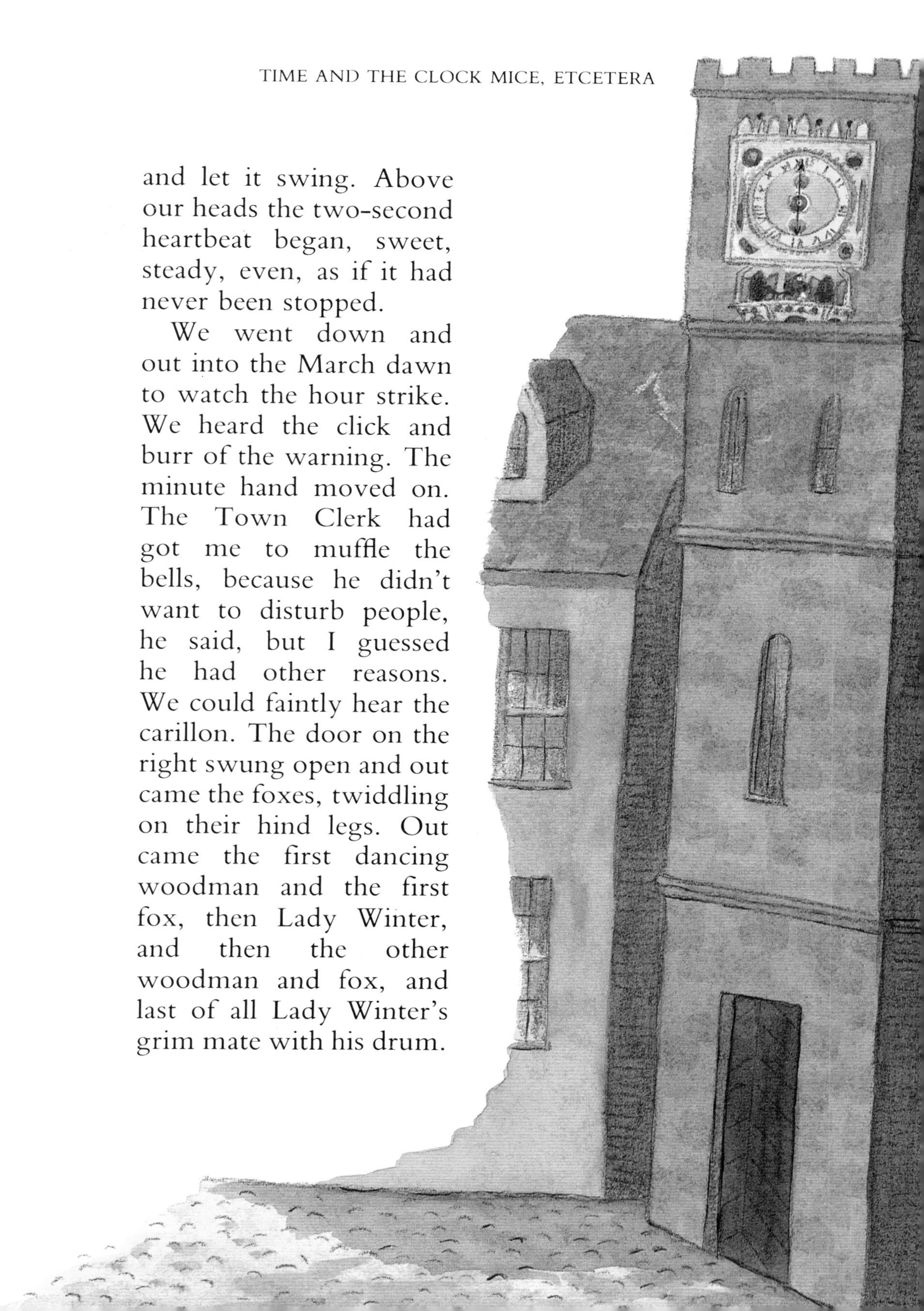

and let it swing. Above our heads the two-second heartbeat began, sweet, steady, even, as if it had never been stopped.

We went down and out into the March dawn to watch the hour strike. We heard the click and burr of the warning. The minute hand moved on. The Town Clerk had got me to muffle the bells, because he didn't want to disturb people, he said, but I guessed he had other reasons. We could faintly hear the carillon. The door on the right swung open and out came the foxes, twiddling on their hind legs. Out came the first dancing woodman and the first fox, then Lady Winter, and then the other woodman and fox, and last of all Lady Winter's grim mate with his drum.

They stopped in the centre and did their dance while the muffled quarters chimed. We waited for the man to beat the drum.

I don't know how I'd expected to muffle Old Joe – I should have disconnected his hammer, but maybe even a little thing like that would have mucked up the balance of the clock – it had got to be all working or none of it would work. Be that as it may, he didn't appreciate having his hammer muffled. I could feel his note resonate along my thigh-bones, a deep, surly boom it seemed without its clank of metal striking on metal.

It won't have been only my thigh-bones that resonated. All round the square the windowpanes, the frames of the beds, the mugs on the trays set out for morning tea, the dentures in the tooth-glasses by the beds, the silver photo-frames round snaps of grandchildren, the very tiles and timbers of the buildings, all of them must have stirred and answered according to their fashion, rattling or groaning or twanging or quivering. The sleepers

too, they stirred, woke, listened, understood, ran to the windows . . .

We heard the sashes fly up, and as the last boom of six died away and Time came swinging out to chase the dancers into their cavern, we heard the cheering.

'That's torn it,' said the Town Clerk. 'Now they'll want a party.'

(There's never been a Town Clerk at Branton who enjoyed spending money.)

They made it into a publicity party to tell the world that Branton Town Hall Clock was running again. They had the papers along, and the radio and TV and all, and what are called 'personalities', and almost anyone they could think of to tickle the interest of tourists. The square was lit and decorated like Christmas twice over, and there was free wine and free beer (while it lasted) and a

barbecue and ices and a band to dance to, and jugglers and clowns and morris men and a pageant of the history of Branton, of which there isn't any. I set the pendulum swinging at 11.55 and everyone got their glass of wine and they counted the noon

strike through, all together, and everyone cheered and threw streamers and the band played and the dancing began, while the nobs and notables went into the Assembly Room for a sit-down dinner. With champagne.

They included me in, which was nice of them. In fact, they did me proud for having got their clock started, and put me on the top table, and they'd even asked me who I'd fancy sitting beside.

'Someone young and pretty,' I said. 'I don't get enough of that, my age.'

(No, there's no fool like an old fool.)

Oh, if I'd met her fifty years before!

Her name was Lilith. She was the Town Clerk's daughter, though you'd never have guessed it to look at them. She was twenty. Pretty isn't in it. Gingery hair in shining waves, and big green eyes flecked brown with an almost-squint (very fetching, I find that), high cheekbones, neat red mouth, a skin you wanted to touch to see if it was real . . . oh, I had excuses for my folly!

She was in the end chair on the top table, with no-one on the other side, so she'd only me to talk to. She didn't seem to mind. She laughed, and listened, and asked questions – the right questions, showing she'd understood. And she was interested in everything, the clock, Grandad, my cats, Cousin

Minnie and her bells and the resonances of the universe, Cousin Angel and her cats, Cousin Cyrus and the rainforests and the marmalade – even my old dad and his airships which I'd never taken much heed of . . .

I told her all that.

She didn't care for champagne, either, so I got her whack on top of mine.

I told her about the mice.

Those big green eyes opened wider still, and shone.

'That's absolutely fascinating,' she said. 'I must tell Michael.'

I felt my heart turn to ice.

'Who's Michael?' I said.

'He's my boyfriend,' she said.

'Well, I'd much rather . . .' I began.

'Oh, but I must,' she said. 'It's just what he's been looking for. He's a research psychologist, you see, teaching rats to run through mazes and finding how quick they learn, but all that's been done before and it'll never make him famous. What he needs is something new. Like telepathic intelligent mice. I bet no-one's worked on anything like that before.'

She rattled on about Michael's career, and how important it was for him to get a good start and publish scientific papers which would make people notice him, while I tried to think. I was sober for a few minutes. I'd always read shock could do that to you, but I'd never believed it. It's true.

My first thought was to tell her I'd been having her on, but I didn't think she'd believe me. Then I thought of refusing to let Michael into the tower, but that wasn't much good. It wasn't my tower, for a start, and Lilith was the Town Clerk's daughter, and we'd got all the TV and newspapers in England right there in Branton hunting for stories. There aren't any stories in Branton, except when the clock stops.

Then I had a much better idea.

'Look,' I said, 'you'd best not tell anyone except Michael. I don't want a lot of people poking around after mice in the clock, upsetting its balance. And you don't want anyone nipping in ahead of him and pinching his research project. Right?'

'Oh, of course not,' she said. 'When can he come?'

I'd need a couple of nights, I thought. Better get it over before the story comes out. We fixed for the day after next.

FOURTH ESSAY ON MICE

Wee, sleekit, cow'rin', tim'rous beastie,
O what a panic's in thy breastie . . .

That's Robert Burns, and it's poppycock!

We're always doing this sort of thing about animals, calling wolves cruel and foxes sly and so on, as if we people were so much kinder and honester ourselves. Your average wolf is as good a parent as a human, more co-operative with the rest of its pack than we are, and so on. All right, they hunt and kill other animals for food. We send other animals to the slaughterhouse for food. I've never heard of wolves killing other animals for fun, but I've met humans who do.

And mice? Of course, they're pretty skilled at keeping out of sight, dodging attacks, scuttling for safety. Wouldn't you be, in a world full of cats and hawks thirty times your size looking for supper?

To my mind it doesn't make sense talking of ordinary mice being brave or timid. They do what they have to do. If they have to fight, they'll fight regardless. It's mainly instinct.

But Clock Mice, who can consider the dangers they're in and their chances one way or other . . .

I tell you, from personal experience, that Clock Mice can be as brave as any human I've ever heard of. Look how Tracy's mum stayed with her litter

the first time I opened Lady Summer's back. Look how they risked their lives, trying to give Jeremy a chance when Juno got him. Look what they did when they understood about my plan.

It wasn't as if they had to. I think it would have worked. But they decided it was wrong.

Wicked? I don't like the word, but well, yes, this time.

Wicked.

I hadn't thought of it like that, of course, not being a mouse. To me it was just a way out of the mess I'd landed us in.

I didn't drink any more champagne, and as soon as the speeches were over (some very nice things they said about me – and Grandad too, apart from forgetting to mention they still hadn't paid for the clock) I slipped away to Ma Palozzi's tea-parlour. The band was still playing, and hundreds of people were dancing, stopping to watch and cheer when the quarters chimed, and to shout the count of hours when the green man banged his drum, and I sat in the window watching them with my heart in my boots, swigging strong Darjeeling and trying to sober up.

The honest truth is, I was ashamed to face the mice.

It was funny. If you'd asked me *how* I was going to tell them, I wouldn't have known. I hadn't even thought about it. All I knew was I'd got to do it.

So at last, with getting on a gallon of tea sloshing round inside me and my ears ringing with the tannin, but still pretty woozy from the champagne, I picked my way through between the dancers and let myself into the tower. It was getting towards evening now, and the mice were beginning to stir for their night-time doings. None of them took much notice of me.

How do you say, 'Hey, folks listen! I've got news for you!' to a bunch of telepathic mice?

I actually said it aloud a few times to passing mice, but they didn't take a blind bit of notice.

Then I got my wits together and started trying to think at them.

How do you think 'listen', without thinking the word itself?

It's a bit like one of those party games where you try to get your team to guess some phrase you've been given ('Look before you leap', 'Please do not adjust your set' – things like that) without saying anything. You draw it, or you act it, depending on the game. You try to make the others *see* it. You make pictures.

'Listen'?

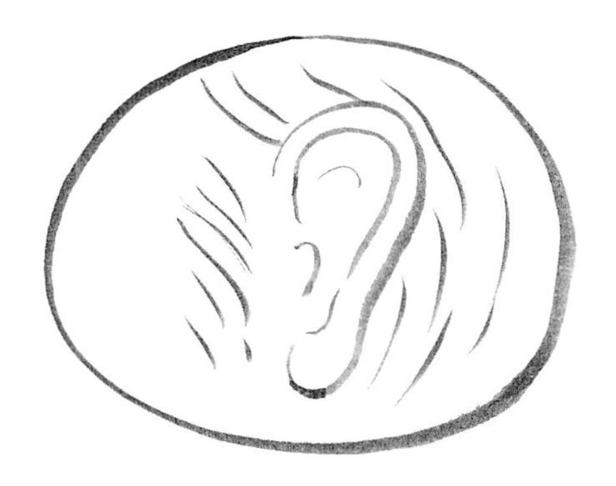

No, of course not.

It's not as easy as you'd think, controlling mind-pictures. You begin to form them and they sort of slither into other things, or just melt, and you find you're thinking in words. I did my best, but not a mouse looked up from its errand to wonder what I was up to, crouching over them, grimacing like a maniac.

I couldn't even get their attention! I thought of opening up one of the nests. Polly Dickory had a new litter and she'd stay while I tried with her, though the other mice seemed to regard her as a bit of a scatterbrain. I was getting a screwdriver out to prize her door open when Tracy came scampering across the floor to see what I was up to.

That's more like it, I thought. If I can't get through to Tracy I can't to any of them, so I picked her up and put her on my palm – she'd let me do that – and held her about fifteen centimetres from my nose.

I thought sad:

I thought difficult:

I thought danger:

She sat there looking at me. Her eyes were as clever as Lilith's in their own mouse way, but I could see I hadn't got through to her.

I thought sorry:

I couldn't keep the pictures clear. I was too sick at myself for being such a fool, just because of a pretty young woman sitting beside me for an hour or two, and me supposed to be seventy-plus sensible.

Tracy put her head on one side, still puzzled, but with a different sort of puzzlement, more like when she'd been watching me at work and trying to fathom out what the bits were for. Then she seemed to make up her mind.

She nipped up my arm and down my suit to the floor. She started across, and turned. Her look said, 'Come along,' as plain as speaking.

She nipped up on to the carousel and started off round the rim. It was about ten minutes to six and I'd been sitting beside Lady Autumn, who'd just come in from her dance with her harvesters and rabbits at the three-quarters strike. Tracy went on past her own home in Lady Summer, past Lady Spring and the Hickory clan, and all the way round to Lady Winter, who was waiting there in the shadows, ready to go out on the hour.

There she stopped. I could feel she was nervous, unsure. Some of the other mice had noticed something was up and had come along to watch.

Tracy seemed to take a breath, as if she'd made up her mind to go through with whatever it was. She went quietly forward to Lady Winter's feet, where she paused for a moment, looking up, then started to climb. The carved leaves of Lady Winter's dress gave her easy footholds the whole way up. She settled on the shoulder, beside the white wooden neck, and looked at me.

'Well?' her look said.

I came closer. I didn't need to say 'Listen' any more, so I started with something I knew I could make a picture of in my mind:

She'd have seen that down in the market, raiding the pet-stalls at night. The mice fancied pet-food more than human food for ordinary eating. Well, they would, wouldn't they?

Tracy stared at me, still puzzled. She knew I was trying to tell her something, but I wasn't getting through. Perhaps mouse brains are the wrong shape for human thoughts.

She cocked her head to Lady Winter, for all the world as if she was saying, 'Can you make anything of this, ma'am?'

I shrugged to myself. Well, why not? If I was crazy enough to try and send mind-pictures to a mouse, it wasn't that much crazier sending them to a block of carved wood. Lady Winter had been sideways to me so far, standing ready to go out and do her dance. I moved round so that I could look straight at the pale, calm, sorrowful face. In the fall of the shadows I couldn't see that her eyeballs were nothing but painted wood.

The pictures seemed to come a bit more orderly into my mind, and didn't slip around. I kept it simple as I could:

That's only a very rough idea of what I thought, and it's taken Emma hours to draw. I made the pictures in my mind, clearer, more detailed, in just a few seconds. And I didn't think jagged edges and things like that. I just thought Warning – Danger, without any words.

Anyway, I was fairly sure I'd made it clear what I was going to do, supposing Tracy was somehow picking it up, using Lady Winter as a sort of interpreter. Over the next two nights I'd catch some ordinary mice in the market, and when Michael came I'd let him think I'd caught them in the tower. He'd do his experiments and not find anything special, and he'd decide I was just a silly old man who'd been trying to impress his Lilith.

Tracy asked me a question. It flicked into my mind, mouse-speed, and out again. It came through Lady Winter. It was as clear as a rap on my own front door. That's how I know about the wavy look they make for questions:

No, I told her:

Then the carillon began. I must have been concentrating so hard on getting my pictures sent that I'd never noticed the warning. I jumped back – I'd been standing just where the door was due to open. The mice – dozens of them by now – scuttered off the carousel.

But Tracy – maybe she'd been as absorbed as I was – stayed put on Lady Winter's shoulder.

'Hold tight,' I shouted, forgetting it wouldn't mean anything to her.

The lugs that held the carousel still between strikes clicked down and the carousel moved smoothly round, taking the foxes and woodmen, Lady Winter with Tracy on her shoulder and the green man out into the open.

I could feel Tracy's fright as she was carried out over the twinkling square, with all the cheering people waiting for the strike. It wasn't them she was frightened of, though. Now that the clock

was going again they must all have begun to get used to being carried out over the square once an hour. I think it was something to do with being out there with Lady Winter when the green man beat the drum.

While the quarters were sounding I went back to the far door, to wait for Lady Winter to carry Tracy back in. Lucky for me I did. I'd forgotten about old Joe. I might have been standing right beside him while he was striking.

I'd never been in the going chamber for that. You remember about the Town Clerk not wanting anyone to know we'd got the clock mended till he was good and ready? So until that day there'd been just that one muffled strike, early in the morning. I wasn't prepared.

Nine miles off you can hear old Joe, given a good wind. So think what it might be like to be standing not five metres from him, inside the same four echoing walls. My hands flew to cover my ears without me telling them, but still the sound shuddered through me. My long bones quivered, my dentures danced on my gums and my skull rang like an answering bell.

Six strokes I endured. If it had been twelve I think I might have been deaf for life, like St Joseph's priest (and no-one was going to make *me* Archbishop of York.) As it was, the ringing didn't go out of my ears till I burnt my tongue on my breakfast sausages two days later. By the time I stopped swearing the ringing was gone. Don't ask me why.

Where was I?

Oh, yes, waiting for Lady Winter to bring Tracy back in. It was all right. She was still there, perched on the carved shoulder. She looked different, dazed – no, *dazed* isn't right, *amazed* is more like it, as if she'd been shown things beyond seeing, told things beyond knowing, been away outside mouse-time and people-time and clock-time and now as the hour-strike ended had been born all over again back into her everyday mouse world.

Or it might have been just the effect of being out there, high up over the square in the sweet spring dusk, with the glitter of lights below and half Branton singing and cheering and counting the strokes. That would have been quite something.

Anyway, in a couple of seconds she shook her fur and became young Tracy again. She glanced at me ('Oh yes, of course, that's what we were on about,') and ran down Lady Winter's dress, flowing over the green leaves like a big drop of tea dribbling down. She settled herself on the white carved toes and all the mice, barring the babies, gathered round in a circle and looked at her. Nothing happened, except maybe in their minds.

I stood and watched with the whine of the

after-strike throbbing in my ears. It struck me that maybe the mice were deaf, what with Old Joe bellowing at them a hundred and fifty-six times a day, day in, day out. That might explain a lot. Deaf mice wouldn't survive a week, you'd think. It's not just the sounds of danger they'd miss, the snuffle of a dog nosing along a pile of cartons, the grate of a footstep. Ordinary mice chatter the whole time, greetings, quarrels, warnings – if we could hear all the way up their voice-range we'd be maddened by their continual squeaking.

Soon as the tower was built there'd have been ordinary mice moving in, what with the market so handy. The babies would have been deaf before they left the nests, so they wouldn't have lived long. But suppose one litter had a parent with an extra gene for mind-casting, and they inherit it, and that does them instead of squeaking and listening, so they get by, and pass the gene on, and that's where Clock Mice come from in the first place . . .

That's how a scientist might look at it. It's one way of slicing the Swiss roll.

I was wondering about this when I noticed the mice stirring. Not much, just their heads moving this way and that, the way you'd see in a group of people if they were arguing something over and all turning together to look at whoever was speaking. The discussion didn't take long, happening in mouse-time, and then they turned back to Tracy. She thought at them for a few seconds more and then flowed back up to Lady Winter's shoulder and looked at me.

I came closer and gazed into the blind wooden eyes, which I'd got Hiram Kapo to paint a nice dark grey only the week before.

She told me NO.

It wasn't a word. It wasn't a picture either. It was a sharp thought in my mind, coming from outside. I knew that without thinking about it, the way you know when you hear your name called from outside the room you're in.

I felt *Oh? But why . . .?*, and maybe she picked that up because she tried to explain:

I didn't get it. She tried again:

I realized the mice didn't think only in pictures. We don't talk only about things we can see, do we? We wouldn't have much worth saying without words like *happy* and *stupid* and *right* and *cheating* and *kind* and so on. I could feel Tracy gearing down, the way you would if you were trying to explain something to a small child. This time she tried pictures:

I got it. She was telling me what my plan was *like*.

It was as if, when Juno had caught Jeremy, instead of trying to trick her away from him themselves, they'd brought their children as bait.

I wanted to argue. It wasn't like that. Some of those children were going to grow into Clock Mice, weren't they? Ordinary mice were different. They didn't matter.

I didn't put it in pictures but she must have got my drift. NO, she told me again, and then:

She let me feel the love that a mother has for *all* her children. What right, she was saying, have we got to let ordinary mice bear our dangers?

I could have gone on. They're just animals, I could have told her. You've got as much right to use them any way you want as people have to use animals the way we do . . .

But I guessed I wasn't going to get the Clock Mice to follow that line of argument. (I'm not sure I follow it myself, sometimes.)

Look, I told her, he's coming. He's dangerous. What are you going to do?

She told me.

SECOND ESSAY ON SCIENCE

Science means knowing. *Scio* = I know. Latin.

How do I know that?

How do I know there was ever a language called Latin, and somebody called Julius Caesar running around in a white sheet and conquering Gaul and getting stabbed by his pals on the Ides of March, whatever they are? How do I know I didn't dream the whole thing up, all the books in the libraries, all the long words in our language. Hadrian's Wall.

Well, I've walked along Hadrian's Wall, haven't I?

Unless I dreamed it.

How do I know I'm not crazy about Romans the same way Cousin Angel is crazy about cats? I say Romans ruled the world once, she says cats. What's the difference? How do I *know*?

I don't.

There is no such thing as knowing, absolutely bang-certain knowing, not even an atom of doubt about it, not even a quark. Look, I've got this goose egg in my hand you've given me, and I'm holding it out of the window and I'm going to let it go, and there's Mrs Curry below cycling off to give her chat to the Over-60s Club about crocheting cuddly toys. How do I know it's *really* going to fall towards the centre of the earth and not stop until it reaches Mrs Curry's bike-basket and goes splat among a lot of fluffy pink rabbits?

I don't. About Mrs Curry, of course, I don't. Look, there's that Mr O'Dowd she's got her eye on coming out of the post office. She'll stop and chat with him, I'll be bound . . . Told you so. She always does, doesn't she?

It doesn't follow, does it? Because Mrs Curry always stops and chats with Mr O'Dowd if she gets the chance, it doesn't *prove* she will this time. I didn't actually *know*.

What's so different about the egg? How do I know it isn't just coincidence that everything anyone's dropped so far has fallen towards the centre of the earth, but it won't happen this time?

Well, of course I know. It's as certain as anything can be. But it still isn't absolutely dead certain.

I think we need two different words, *Know* and *Qnow*.

Know is for ordinary knowing, the sort we all get along with. *Qnow* is for absolutely dead certain knowledge, which you can never have.

So, OK, science is knowing. The trouble is, scientists keep trying to turn it into qnowing. Just one little bit more knowledge, they think, and we'll have qnowledge.

And that makes anything they do all right. They think.

Lilith's Michael was a pleasant young man, almost good enough for a girl like her, enjoyed country walks, collected old milking stools for a hobby, played the accordion for a folk-group Tuesdays, called me 'Sir' which I pretend not to bother with but which makes me think I'm still some use in the world.

I tried to open the door with the wrong keys and let him find the right one and do it for me, and then I went muttering and snuffling up ahead of him so he could get a good look at my feet because I was wearing one slipper and one boot.

The going-chamber was a right mess. I'd dropped crusts and apple-cores around and the mice had nibbled and messed with them, and left their own droppings the way ordinary mice do, and bits of stuff they might have been dragging up for nests and so on.

I offered Michael coffee from my Thermos and it turned out a mixture of tea and cocoa, tepid, and I mumbled about how I must have forgotten to empty the old tea out before I put the coffee in, which somehow I'd gone and made of cocoa, and he laughed and said it was a new experience, at least, and how about catching some mice as it looked as if there were plenty around.

He'd brought three cunning little traps which wouldn't hurt the mice, and he baited them with bits of apple and we swept up the other leavings

so the mice wouldn't have anything else to go for, and we left it like that.

He came again next morning. All three traps had mice in them – Terry Hickory, Tracy Dickory and Sebastian Dock. He picked up the one with Sebastian and looked at him.

'Looks like your average House Mouse,' he said. 'I can't see any difference.'

He was right there. They looked a lot dumber than ordinary mice, even. If there'd been Oscars for acting thick, those three would have won them.

'Well, thank you, sir,' he said. 'Why don't you come along to the lab next week and you can see how they're making out.'

A week. Months, in mouse time. Months in prison. I couldn't tell him that so I got my diary out and we fixed a day and I wrote it down in the wrong month and let him put me right. I watched from above while he buzzed out of the square in one of those little open cars men like him drive.

I was afraid.

I'd no more business in Branton beyond waiting to see whether the Council would find a way of not paying me, so I drove over to visit Cousin Minnie.

'So you've got your clock going?' she said.

'Heard it all on the telly, did you?' I said.

'I knew before that,' she said. 'Soon as the big bell struck noon, I knew.'

'Ah, come off it,' I said. 'It's forty-five miles if it's an inch.'

'I didn't say I heard him,' she said. 'I felt my bells move to his sounding.'

I shrugged. Everyone to their own nonsense. Live and let live.

'What's the matter with you?' she said. 'You're not right with yourself, are you?'

'I'm afraid,' I said, and I told her what had happened, from the beginning. I was still ashamed of myself to the soles of my shoes, but I didn't leave anything out. She didn't say anything till I got to the bit about being stuck in the tower while Old Joe was striking.

'Won't do you much harm,' she said. 'He might even have banged some sense into you. That's a marvellous great bell you've got there. No wonder your mice are brighter than most.'

'You could be right,' I said, and told her my idea about the bell making the mice deaf and so forcing them telepathic.

'That's just like you,' she said. 'Some ways you're blinder than I am. If you'd any feel for the nature of things you'd understand about the resonances of the universe embodying themselves in a bell like that, and changing things round about as they pulse back where they came.'

'You're talking like Cousin Angel,' I said.

'Don't you go despising Cousin Angel,' snapped Minnie. 'I know she can't toast a crumpet or boil an egg so that anyone would want to eat them, but you'll be glad of her before the week's over.'

I laughed at her, and we had our usual row about the nature of things, and that cheered us both up. I finished telling her about Michael while I was eating a few baps for tea, and went home to be with my cats.

Michael worked at Yatterby University, I forgot to say. I meant to get early to the lab and then apologize for being late, but I was late anyway, having got caught up in a student protest about having to live in sewerpipes instead of houses because the money had run out.

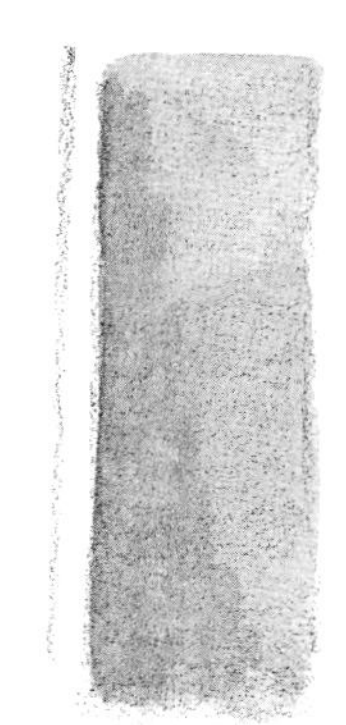

The receptionist pretended not to notice I was still wearing my pyjamas under my jacket, so maybe Michael had told her what to expect, or maybe they get a lot of crazy old professors doddling about so I wasn't anything out of the normal.

Michael came and signed me through the security system. It was like getting into some kind of world-domination power-plant, with steel grilles, electronic tags, guards, armoured doors with codes to punch before they'd open, the lot.

'It's the animal liberation people,' Michael explained. 'They keep trying to break in and set the experimental animals free. People don't seem to understand that we treat our animals as well as possible here, because it's worth our while. You can't work with sick animals. And if you let them loose outside they'd be dead in a week. Look at those rats, for instance . . .'

I hadn't even recognized the things in the cage as rats. They were horrible. They hadn't a hair on them.

'What's happened to them?' I said. 'Have they been shaved?'

'That would be some job,' he said. 'I've trouble enough with my own chin. No, they're a special inbred strain with defective genes in the part of the chromosome that codes for hair. Dr Pollard is studying the defect.'

The bald rats looked perfectly happy, I've got to admit. Their eyes were bright, their noses twitched, they scampered or dozed. They were still horrible.

Michael took me on to the section where he worked. He showed me a black-and-white rat in a cage. There were three buttons for it to poke with its nose. If it got them in the right order a bell rang and a scrap of food came out of a tube, but if it tried the same order twice it got an electric shock. Michael was studying how long it took for it to learn the rules for finding the new right order

each time. He said some rats got it in three days but some never made it because they had nervous breakdowns first. There was a machine by the cage to count the tries so he didn't have to stand and watch it happening.

I told him I thought it was a very interesting experiment. I didn't tell him I meant it was interesting about people, not about rats.

There were other cages of rats and mice, some doing experiments, some just loafing around. Michael was gentle with them when he picked them up, stroking the backs of their heads and murmuring to them. They weren't at all afraid of him.

The Clock Mice were over in a cupboard by themselves. Michael said he had to keep them separate from the others because they'd come in from the wild and they'd be carrying infections which the lab mice didn't have any resistance to. I looked at them eagerly. They seemed all right, though they pretended not to recognize me.

'What do you make of them?' I said. 'Bright, aren't they?'

He looked at me with that special sort of patience which clever young men keep for old fools. I knew we were winning.

'Well,' he said. 'Judge for yourself. We'll try them on the see-saw.'

He pulled out from under the table a flat wooden box without a lid. In the middle was a sort of see-saw, mouse-size, but with one end of the plank longer than the other. A bit of wire with a hook on the end was arranged so that the hook was directly over the short end of the see-saw. Michael stuck a piece of apple on the hook and lifted Tracy and Terry out of their cages and put them in the box.

'See how it works?' he said. 'A mouse can reach the apple from the top of the see-saw, but only if the other mouse stays at the bottom and keeps it weighed down. So it depends on them learning to co-operate. I thought it would be a good test to see if there's anything like telepathy going on. I may as well tell you that a pair of my lab rats will usually get the hang of it in two or three minutes. So let's see. This isn't their first try by any means.'

Terry started off by trying to climb out, but the box had a rim to stop this and he kept falling off. The third time he fell on Tracy, who'd been sitting scratching herself, but now looked up and peered at

the ceiling, as if she thought it might go on raining mice. Then she pretended to notice the apple for the first time. She gave a squeak of excitement and shot up the see-saw, which of course tilted under her weight and sent her tumbling down the other side. Immediately she circled round and tried again, and again, and again, like a clockwork toy. At first Terry went on trying to climb out, but then he too noticed the apple and joined in, timing his dash for the see-saw so that he collided with Tracy at the bottom. They had a classic mouse spat, struggling for who should be first. Terry won, but Tracy came close behind him so that they both went tumbling and swearing down the other side.

They kept that up for a bit, but then they let themselves become separated out so that by the time one of them reached the bottom of the see-saw it was already tilting out of reach and they had to wait for it to fall back. Then Terry half caught up with Tracy, so that he reached the bottom just before the see-saw tilted and his weight kept it in place until she'd almost reached the apple.

All at once she seemed to realize he was following her up. She turned and swore at him, and he backed off down to the bottom of the see-saw. Gingerly she edged up the slope again.

'Look,' I whispered. 'They've got it!'

But just as Tracy was squatting up to reach for the apple Terry yawned and let go of the see-saw, and Tracy thumped down.

Michael laughed. I managed to keep a straight face, just.

'That's about par for the course,' he said. 'They

do sometimes fluke it but they just don't learn. It's the same with the mazes and all the other tests. In fact, on average they perform markedly worse than lab-bred mice.'

I shook my head and tried to look downcast. Good little Tracy, I thought. Well done, Terry and Sebastian. We'll soon have you out of here and home in your nests and it will all be over and no harm done, except for Michael deciding I'm a silly old fool, which I am, but not in the way he thinks.

'But there is something curious about them,' he said.

'Uh?' I said. That wasn't so good.

'I noticed it a couple of days back,' he said. 'I put them in separate cages so that the males didn't fight. Mostly they're just like other mice, nosing around and eating and sleeping. But sometimes they lie still, with their eyes open, and when they do that they all do it at the same time. It's more curious because they can't see each other.'

Oh, Lor, I thought, that's torn it. They've been talking to each other, and he's noticed. Bright of him. He'd go far, spotting something like that.

'Then I remembered you'd said something to Lilith about them being what you called telepathic,' he said. 'I don't believe in that sort of thing, as usually presented, but it looked as if some sort of communication might be taking place.'

'You wouldn't hear them,' I said. 'Their voices are out of our range.'

'I rigged mikes and checked on that,' he said. 'In fact, they vocalize much less than normal mice . . .'

'It's because they're wild,' I managed to say. 'They don't want to give themselves away to cats and things.'

'Possibly,' he said. 'Still, it's a puzzle. There must be an explanation like that. I'll know a bit more when I've taken a look at their brains.'

'A look at their brains?' I said.

He looked up from putting the mice back into their cages.

'That's right,' he said.

'A. Look. At. Their. Brains?'

'Don't worry,' he said. 'It's absolutely painless. I put them down with an injection, and . . .'

'You can't do that,' I said.

'I do it all the time,' he said. 'It's the normal procedure. They're just mice.'

'They aren't just mice!' I said.

That's wrong. I can't have said it. I must have yelled or bellowed or screamed it, the way he was looking at me. I felt as if my hair was standing on end. Beyond his elbow I saw Terry and Tracy and

Sebastian looking at me too, bright-eyed, themselves, not acting dumb. That pulled me together a bit. I realized I was on the edge of telling Michael the truth, and if I did that nothing would stop him in his lust for Qnowledge, and he'd tell the world. He was almost there now. There was a sharp look in his eyes, as though he'd guessed I wasn't as batty as I'd been making out, and I was keeping something from him.

'What do you mean, not just mice?' he said.

I remembered just in time what Cousin Minnie had told me about Cousin Angel coming to the rescue. If she could worship cats, then I could worship mice.

I fell to my knees. I knocked my forehead on the ground in front of the three cages.

'Forgive him, oh, forgive him his blasphemy!' I

cried. 'Listen young man! What you see before you may look to you like common mice, but I tell you that they are emanations of the Mouse-God of the ancient Egyptians, the great God Pteek! If you hurt one whisker of their heads the most dreadful curses will fall on you for the rest of your life. There will be thunderstorms at all your picnics and computer errors in your tax accounts and cows will stampede across your rosebeds and Lilith will have hiccups at romantic moments and your car will make strange untraceable grinding noises and there will be wood-worm in your milking-stools and your accordion will leak and wherever you go on holiday your luggage will fetch up in Vancouver and your video won't record anything except *Neighbours* and your

children won't think about anything but money . . .'

I was gibbering by now. I'd run out of curses but I kept right on gibbering. Michael took me by the hands and pulled me to my feet.

'Look,' he said gently. 'It's not a big deal. Why don't you just tell me you don't want them put down because they're your pet mice?'

I managed to say it without snarling. They weren't mine. They weren't pets. They were Terry, Tracy and Sebastian.

'They're my pet mice. Please let me have them back.'

'Yes, of course, sir. I'm sorry. I didn't realize.'

He found a box for me and we put the mice in it and I took them home.

FIFTH ESSAY ON CLOCKS

Clocks aren't time.

It's an easy mistake to make, because clocks measure time – measure one sort of time, I mean. We listen to the steady way tock follows tick and tick follows tock and we watch the cogs turning, each tooth meshing where it must and nowhere else, this causing that and that causing t'other, cause and effect plain to see if you know what you're looking for . . .

But time's not really like that. Time's strange.

I sent Lilith and Michael a wedding-present, a little clock I made specially for them. It's in a glass case so that you can see all the works, and how they mesh and function – and then all of a sudden you say to yourself, 'That's nonsense. That can't work. That wheel's going the wrong way.' And it is. But the clock tells the time OK.

It's a trick, of course. I made it like that on purpose. I'm not going to tell Michael how it works, and I'm not going to tell him why I gave it to him, either. I just want him to understand that there'll always be things he can't know.

Time's one of those things. We'll never understand it. Our minds are born into it. We live by it, one breath following another. We can never get outside to see what it is. I've read somewhere that there's no good reason why time flows in the direction it does – it could just as well go the other way, what we'd call backwards. What does that mean? Don't ask me. I know pretty well everything there is to know about clocks, but I don't understand time.

I'm getting to the end of mine, now. Maybe in that last moment, as I slip out of it, I'll be allowed to look back over it from outside and say to myself, 'Oh, of course! *Now* I see!'

Meanwhile we've all got to get along with time, best we can. It's where we're at. Maybe that's why we like stories, because they show us time happening – they're a sort of practice at time. We're outside *their* time.

How long has it taken you to read this story? Couple of hours (half that, if you skipped the bits like this)? But it took seven months to happen, and you were outside those months in your couple of hours.

And it isn't finished yet. That's another thing about stories – they have ends. Time doesn't. Happy ever after? Ever after? Till the stars fold in on themselves, the way they will one day – only there won't be any days because long before that the sun will have gone giant and swallowed the earth and then it will have gone small and become a spinning dot, hurtling round hundreds of times a minute, only there won't be any minutes . . .?

All right, all right, stories have ends. Let's finish.

I took the mice back and we all heaved a sigh of relief. Then I went away for a break, telling people I was going into a rest-home because I'd had some sort of a breakdown brought on by overwork getting the clock finished in time for the opening. (That was to account for my dealings with Lilith and Michael.) I showed George Baff's nephew how to wind the weights up and told him he wasn't to touch another thing.

I went home and fussed over my cats, who I'd been neglecting. Then I found a lawyer, a really bright woman who got my drift at once and told me what to say. I went back to Branton good and ready to have it out with the Town Clerk.

I caught him on the hop. Michael must have told Lilith about me going gaga, and Lilith had told her dad, so he wasn't expecting to find me with all my marbles in place and every penny counted. It came to a tidy sum.

They never like spending money, Town Clerks.

I couldn't ask him to settle Grandad's bill – that was too late, in law – but I said I wanted to see some sort of justice done. I still had Grandad's plans, and I was the only man in the world who understood how the clock worked. (I wasn't lying. Tracy's a mouse, and female with it.) I was getting on, I said. They'd need me to teach someone how to take care of the clock when I was gone, right?

A very fair bargain I offered him. They'd settle my bill without question, and I'd put the money into a Trust. I didn't need it – I'm rolling, thanks to some of the things my dad invented for his airships.

The airships themselves were a flop, but some of the bits and bobs turned out really useful for other things – the pump that pumps the hot water round in your central heating, and the special switches on the traffic-lights at the end of your road, for instance . . .

Where was I?

Oh yes, the Trust. The clock itself went into the Trust, and the plans, and the money they owed me, and the money they'd get from marketing T-shirts and things and letting the clock be used in telly-ads, and so on. Minnie and me were trustees, being Grandad's heirs, with power to appoint our successors, and – this is what really mattered – power to choose a clock-keeper.

It was only a part-time job but more than forty people answered our ad. We chose the likeliest four and took them up to the going-chamber in turn, pretending it was to let them see what the job involved. There was one young woman, Donna Lacey, a single mum with twins. She didn't know a thing about clocks but I liked the look of her and Minnie liked the sound of her.

She stood in the going-chamber and stared at the dancers, all of them still in their between-strikes poses.

'Ever since I was tiny I've wanted to come up here and see them close,' she said. 'I was born just across the square. I used to watch them from my bedroom window when I was supposed to be asleep. I still think Lady Winter's the most beautiful thing in the world. And I suppose this is Old Joe.'

'Fetch him a biff,' said Minnie. 'Don't be afraid. Harder than that.'

Donna did as she was told and thumped the dead metal with the side of her fist, and the bell woke and answered with its intertwining voices, something I could never make happen though I'd hit it pretty well every time I passed.

'She'll do,' said Minnie. 'She was born with his ringing in her bones.'

'But I told you I don't know anything about clocks,' said Donna. 'I just wanted the chance to come and look at the dancers.'

'You don't have to know anything,' I said.

I opened Lady Summer's back and Tracy skipped out on to my hand and I took her round and put her on Lady Winter's shoulder. I stood Donna where she could look into Lady Winter's eyes.

Nothing happened for a bit. Then she laughed.

'I see,' she said. 'She's going to be the clock-keeper. I'm just the assistant.'

'That's right,' I said.

She chatted away to Tracy for a while, telling her about her children.

And Tracy told her about her brother Kevin untying one of the balloon-seller's souvenir balloons and nearly getting carried away to Gloag, and her Uncle Will starting to build a grand piano, and how she was going to marry Sebastian next week, and Uncle Gerald having a fight with old Peter Hickory over Madeline. . .

I haven't room for all of it. Tracy's a lovely mouse, but she does talk. Donna took to the idea at once. She seemed to find it much easier than I did – I was never any good at foreign languages, when I was at school.

'Enjoying yourself?' I said.

'Oh, it's so exciting!' said Donna. 'I never imagined. Only don't they think quick!'

'They've got to,' I said, and I explained about mouse time.

'I see,' said Donna. 'Only, well, what happens . . . I mean, how long does a mouse live?'

'Ordinary mice, about three years. But old Ezra

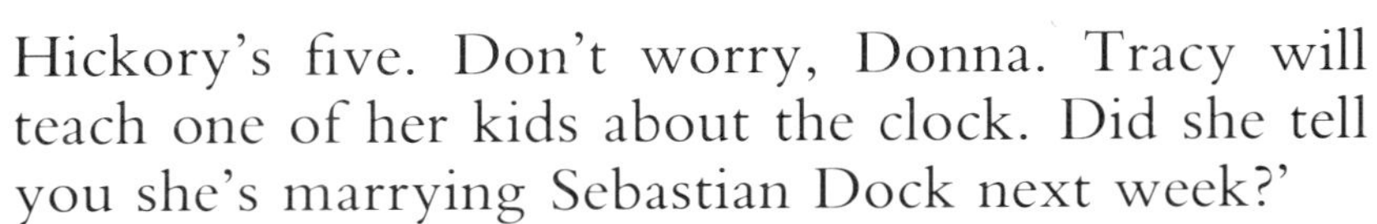

Hickory's five. Don't worry, Donna. Tracy will teach one of her kids about the clock. Did she tell you she's marrying Sebastian Dock next week?'

'She's asked me to the wedding,' said Donna. 'I'll have to get a babysitter. I said I'd make her some cheese straws. Isn't it lucky I'm not afraid of mice?'

LAST ESSAY ON MICE, CLOCKS, BELLS, PEOPLE, SCIENCE, ETCETERA, ESPECIALLY ETCETERA

It came to me in the middle of the night. My age, you wake quite a bit. So I was lying there with my head full of nothing, when all of a sudden I began to wonder if the Branton Town Hall Clock wasn't a bit like this old earth of ours, with its seasons, and the way it's all got to balance to keep going, and bits of it we'll never understand, and us messing around with it not knowing what we're doing, and us sharing it with things like mice, and it needing them as much as it needs us, and all that.

Maybe that's what Grandad meant, building his clock the way he did.

Think about it.